BACKWATER
MYSTIC BLUES

➤◄

BACKWATER
MYSTIC BLUES

➤ ⬅

LLOYD RATZLAFF

thistledown press

Library and Archives Canada Cataloguing in Publication

Ratzlaff, Lloyd, 1946-
Backwater mystic blues / Lloyd Ratzlaff.

ISBN 1-897235-08-9

I. Title.

PS8585.A853B33 2006   C818'.603   C2006-903736-1

Cover painting by Kathy Lindgren
Cover and book design by Jackie Forrie
Typeset by Thistledown Press
Printed and bound in Canada

Thistledown Press Ltd.
633 Main Street
Saskatoon, Saskatchewan, S7H 0J8
www.thistledownpress.com

Thistledown Press gratefully acknowledges the financial assistance of the Canada Council for the Arts, the Saskatchewan Arts Board, and the Government of Canada through the Book Publishing Industry Development Program for its publishing program.

 Canadian Patrimoine
Heritage canadien

 Canada Council   Conseil des Arts
for the Arts   du Canada

ACKNOWLEDGEMENTS

Many thanks to Thistledown Press for including *Backwater Mystic Blues* in its publishing program; and especially to Seán Virgo, editor and good-neighbour-at-large, for his "first, fierce and generous reading" of the manuscript.

Thanks to Kathy Lindgren for lending her watercolour as the cover image. To Maureen Weber for her continuing trust. To the Saskatchewan Arts Board for the boost of a creative grant. To the Saskatchewan Writers Guild for their sabbaticals known as Colonies; and for granting first prize to "Requiem" in the 2004 Short Manuscript Awards, and honourable mention to "Queen of Clubs" in 2005.

Early versions of some of these pieces appeared in *The Harpweaver*, *NewWest Review*, *Prairie Messenger*, *Rhubarb*, *Spring*, and *Wildflower*; and in Black Moss Press's *Letting Go: An Anthology of Loss and Survival*.

Deepest gratitude to Larraine, my partner; to my daughters and sons-in-law, Shannon and Ramsy Unruh and Sheri and Rob Porrelli; and to my grandchildren, Katy, Tom, Nik, Jane, Tate, and Aviana — *Namaste!*

This is a work of literary non-fiction, but some names and details have been altered for discretionary reasons.

CONTENTS

9 Prologue

Religion and Glory

12 Springfield
15 Water Carrier
19 The Bush
23 Cleavage
29 Plastic Flower

Walking Up the Stair

40 The Man Who Wasn't There
45 Concrete Heavens
50 To See in a Sacred Manner
54 The G-word
60 Carling's Gospel
65 Balaam's Ass
69 Three Churches
73 An Improbable Sunshine
83 Making Peace
87 The Salvation of Harvey Nicotine
91 Arul Luthra's Yard
96 Wings

The Play of Forces

104 The Heart of the Matter
108 Mail
112 What the Soul Knows
116 Queen of Clubs
124 Ticket to Heaven
129 Requiem

139 Epilogue

For my parents

PROLOGUE

POWWOW ½ MILE. At the hand-drawn cardboard sign I turn from the grid road near Wanuskewin, follow a bumpy track over the prairie, and park at the far end of a long row of cars. I stroll among wailing children and unhurried adults, and their dogs, and climb up to the bleachers. And sit, one of three white faces in the crowd, waiting for the powwow to begin.

Beside the empty space, a cluster of men sits on the earth around a drum. They test the instrument's skin with their sticks, and in a moment the pounding has begun.

The dancers enter the ring, elders and youngsters together, making their way slowly around the centre pole, some in elaborate headdress, all in a jubilation of colours. The drummers' voices scale and fall — *hi-ya, hey-you, don't be left out.* Newcomers join by ones and twos, a half-dozen partners join abreast and revolve in slow radial sweeps, stepping fancy to the urgency of the singers' cries and the drum's steadfast beat. The hair rises on my neck, my heart throbs in rhythm, and the circle fills until it brims with colour.

Then, a young woman and her child — she in a loose skirt and long white shawl twirling around her daughter, enfolding as if with wings. The girl laughs up into her mother's face, or opens to the dazzle of hues around her.

I watch the dance, entranced for an hour. And on my way back to the car, a bright copper penny winks at me from the ground.

I know what the backwater kid meant when he said to his friend: Once you've been to a circus, you'll never enjoy prayer meeting again.

Religion *and* Glory

SPRINGFIELD

ALBERT AND ELSIE DID OWN A CAR, but it was old and unreliable. Life in the post-depression years of the 1940s was lean, and they were renting a farm in the Springfield district, two miles from each of their parents' homesteads. They had been married for seven years, and only now were expecting their first child.

On a November 1946 morning when Elsie's labour began, they hurried to her parents' farm to pick up a newer model Nash, and flew toward City Hospital forty miles distant. They nearly hit another car en route, and arrived in Saskatoon only to realize they didn't know how to find the hospital, so stopped to ask for directions. When Elsie was finally admitted, Albert went to a washroom to shave — he'd taken his razor kit along — and found a son already born when he returned to the ward.

In the Mennonite community of Springfield and the surrounding villages, when winter set in, most people put their cars up on blocks, for the roads became impassable and stayed so until spring. One mid-December day,

Albert took Elsie and the child to his in-laws', the Glieges', in a horse-drawn sleigh, and went on to do some business in the village of Laird, six miles over the fields as the crow flew.

Elsie and her older sisters, Emma and Anne, who still lived at home, began an annual Christmas-baking bee with their mother. During the afternoon, Emma took a batch of cookies out to the summer kitchen — a small hut where meals were prepared in hot weather to keep the house cool, serving also as a freezer in winter — and hastened back inside to tell Elsie, "Things don't look right at your place."

Elsie telephoned the neighbours nearest to her farm, who confirmed that the house was on fire, and that some men were already on hand to help. She called the railway station in Laird, where Albert was to pick up some freight from the weekly train. When he heard the news, he whipped his horses from the village toward the smoke billowing on the horizon. A few miles into the country he saw how the animals laboured, and felt sorry for them; and seeing that the house was lost anyway, he relented.

In her parents' house, Elsie carried the baby to an upstairs bedroom and looked across the pasture and fields at her burning home, and thought, "Everything's gone, now what?"

Only a dresser and a buffet were rescued from the fire, and a small glass lion that Elsie had received from her parents on her thirteenth birthday.

The next morning, Albert moved their four cows to the in-laws' place, and Elsie scrubbed out a granary in which they thought they'd have to live through the winter. They ended up staying in a guest bedroom of the Gliege house as they tried to rebuild their lives; and at nights, Anne and Emma took turns rocking the baby to sleep.

The community rallied with gifts of food and blankets and odd pieces of furniture, and a few donations of a dollar or two — substantial money in their nearly-cashless society. When a garage in the village of Laird came up for sale, Albert and two of his younger brothers arranged financing, and under a British-American gasoline sign, opened for business. The first winter they sold scarcely ten gallons of gas. They heated the building and brewed coffee for customers, who brought small gadgets for repair but wanted mainly to pass the time in the snowbound village until spring.

When winter was over, Elsie and Albert purchased a small two-storey house in the village of Hepburn, and moved it to Laird; and with their firstborn child, who was me, set up a new home.

This house, this village and field of springs, is where my memories begin.

WATER CARRIER

OUR PORCH, which opened directly into the kitchen, contained only a washing machine driven by a Kohler gasoline engine. In the kitchen itself, there was a coat closet on one side of the door; and on the other, the party-line telephone that reminded me always of a face: its silver bells bulged like eyes at the top, a mouthpiece protruded like a long knobbly nose, the shelf below suggested a chin, and the receiver hung like a distended ear on the left. When someone phoned for us, the face rang *longg-short-longg*. A white cupboard stood against that wall with cooking pots on its lower shelves, and above them, our cups and bowls stacked beside a Nabisco shredded-wheat box. The table along the opposite wall was covered with leftover linoleum from the floor.

Two south windows let the sunshine into the room, and between them stood a low sink with a cold water tap. Hot water came from the reservoir of the Enterprise cookstove opposite. Outside, under the windows, some men once dug a hole and buried the skeleton of a Whippet car body, to prevent our sewer from caving in.

At night I felt eerie looking out there, as if we had a grave beside our house, half-full of putrid black water.

A narrow door opened from the kitchen to the cellar stairs, and the way down was dark and steep. Coarse shelves had been built on the left. The cellar itself was a dismal underworld with three walls of dank earth, and one cement side with a tiny window overhead looking out to the west. Under the stairs, a pressure pump was mounted on the cistern; it was a noisy contraption that began chugging whenever the tap was opened in the kitchen, and stopped with a grunt when the tap was closed. A tawny oil stove hung from the joists by metal straps, like a fat man's pants from his suspenders. The one naked light bulb scarcely lit the cellar's dim edges, where other shelves stood with crocks and jars and bronze canning tubs, where potatoes mouldered in the bin in the northeast, darkest, corner; and the upright hulk of the metal bathtub brooded of Saturdays, when it was wrestled up through the passageway so we could take turns bathing for church on Sunday.

After I began school, it was my duty to take a bucket from the shelf in the cellar stairs and fetch our drinking water from the village well. The prairie came ranging from beyond the streets into our yard, through the shallow ditch in front and from the alley behind, and surrounded our garden and woodpile, and the porch with its orange-crate nailed to the north wall as a milkbox.

The neighbouring yard belonged to the Imperial Bank manager. His residence was three times the size of ours, and featured the only attached garage in town. Around it grew a verdant lawn with flourishing shrubs, and a thick hedge that divided our properties one from the other.

The village well was two blocks away, between Kenny Zulauf's backyard fort and a small lilac bush. The pump was nailed to a wooden cover with crooked, rusty spikes. When I got there, I would step onto the weathered lid and hang my pail from the spout — which had a little cast-iron horn to prevent it from slipping off — and begin the wrangle.

The pump was a reluctant beast, so stiff that I dangled from the iron handle to pull it down, let it rise part-way on its own and dragged it back again before it got too high, and so forced it sluggishly up to a prime — I was tired already — then tried to keep a rhythm going for another hundred ups-and-downs to fill the thirsty pail. The pump squealed and brayed and snorted water, and I snatched quick breaks to rest without losing the prime, and shuddered to think of the wooden lid collapsing and dropping me down, down.

I lugged the water back to our house, panting and blowing, shifting the bucket from hand to hand and sloshing liquid over the sides at each pass; or stoitering ahead with it hanging under my legs and spilling more over my shoes, so that a third of the water might be lost by the time I reached the banker's green hedge.

I carried my pail resolutely through the kitchen, with the telephone bells goggling as I went, lifted the latch of the cellar door and went three steps down. Set the pail on the shelf beside an enamel cup, dipped out a measure of water,and gulped it off.

In my home in the city, I keep the old cup near me on an office shelf. I salvaged it long ago from my parents' house. I like the way my index finger curls perfectly through the flat round handle on the side; and above, how my thumb fondles the smooth coat of paint concealing the solderer's beads. I like the chips in the enamel that reveal a dark metal beneath.

Once in a while, when I'm poised in some new passage between the light and the gloomy chill, I take the vessel and fill it to the top of its wide blue brim. It holds the innocence of childhood, and the taste of clean cold tin straight to the gut slakes my soul, and puts Time in its place.

THE BUSH

THERE WERE TWO WAYS INTO THE BUSH. One was through the ditch of the correction line, where weeds and reeds grew as tall as I was; and at their densest spot I had to jump over a mud bottom to the other side, where the brush began. But a barbwire fence stood in the way, and I had to pass through it like a woman through a magician's knives, only I often had a rip in my pants to show for it later.

The other way led through the pasture, with its notorious bull that might charge at any time. Not that he ever did, but he *could*— and this was another deterrent. So sometimes I skulked along the carragana hedge at the north until the beast looked the other way, and beelined over to the dugout that lay between me and this side of the bush. My older cousins had built a raft from leftover boards and railway ties, and kept it tethered to a post at the water's edge. They used it sometimes to dive from the middle of the dugout, when they weren't off shooting gophers or working in the fields.

I often untied the raft and paddled it across to the fescue and willows on the other side, then disembarked, and found a trail that went snaking through the saplings into the heart of the bush.

There, in a clearing a little bigger than the raft, a flat oval stone protruded from the ground. It was speckled with moss and rust, and a few bluebells hung from their stalks around it. I sat on the rock as the poplar leaves overhead *fuschelled* to the passing breeze, and I could look out from the thicket, though no one from the road or farmyard or pasture could see me.

Sometimes a bee bummelled into the hideout, and out again over the trees, or a raven lit on a branch, rattled the bell in its throat and took off. Alfalfa scents wafted through the undergrowth, or the dark smell of loam summerfallow when the breeze shifted. Frogs burped from the dugout, woodpeckers tapped at a hollow tree near the fence; and when Hungarian partridges burst from the east stubble field they set my heart tapping too.

My father had been raised on this farm. He and his two younger brothers had sold their garage in Laird, and were breaking new land on a river flat three miles to the west, where roots lay scattered over the fields waiting to be picked off. Our families kept a fish-basket hidden in the river, so that anyone working the land could haul the wire hoop onto the bank, and sometimes find a dozen jackfish or goldeyes swirling inside as it came rolling up from the water.

Two miles north of the bush was the farm where my mother had grown up, with its field of thirteen springs that gave the district its name. Other cousins lived there now, and we often swam in the creek beneath a wooden bridge, or stood in the cattle-tunnel under the road and yelled at the cows having a heyday in the thigh-high grass, and heard our echoes bounce from the rough-mortared walls. Bulrushes grew high in the marsh, and in the evenings the bog made me scared of being sucked underwater, underground. On the bank of the creek, my cousin Rueben and I once secretly boiled a can of barley from his granary. We had heard that beer was made this way, and needed it to go with our dry-leaf cigarettes rolled in brown wrapping paper; but it all tasted foul, and we wondered what the real things would be like.

The village of Laird, where I lived, was five miles away. Jane Hardy lived there too, and in school she sat one row over and three desks back. She was the most enchanting creature on earth. My rock in the bush had enough room for the two of us, if she had wanted to come. I didn't know what we'd do together, but wished for a chance to find out — she had secrets to tell, or show me. But I didn't ask, and Jane didn't come; and sometimes I sat in the bush hearing no sounds but those I made myself. Or I watched passersby on the grid road to the south: one in a blue Buick with chrome to set the church talking, another in a buggy with springs under the seat but no rubber on the wheels, as his long-bearded Holdeman sect required.

Across the correction line and two telephone poles down, was Salem Mennonite Church. Salem meant peace, but the revival preachers scared me with invisible Beings: God and Satan, angels and demons — and even our ancestors in the graveyard where the wind sighed in the pines, they could see us too.

High above Springfield and Laird, up beyond the blue, was Heaven. The Blackwood Brothers often sang about it on my uncle's gramophone: *I heard a great thunder* up in the sky, must've been the Saviour passing by. And far below was the other place that started with H: *heard a great rumble under the ground, musta bin the Devil bouncin' up and down.*

Over in church the people sang, *This world is not my home, I'm just a-passing through.* But sometimes, sitting on my rock in the bush, I felt as if I had been there forever, and the world was passing through.

CLEAVAGE

FOR A WHILE WHEN I WAS ELEVEN OR TWELVE, I had a collection of *Star Weekly* pinups on the wall beside my bed. I lived in "town" (as we called the village — and Uncle Harry even liked to call me "city slicker"), and my farm cousins were amazed at this glistering display of idols. Debbie Reynolds was up there, and the McGuire Sisters, and Elvis in whitebucks with a guitar slung back and knees knocking together, arms stretched in a feral pose. Of course, some of the stars looked quite decent: Ricky Nelson, Pat Boone, and Sandra Dee with her bright smile and elegant gown.

But our Sunday School teacher had distributed a pamphlet titled ELVIS WAS MY IDOL, in which a girl confessed that she had *experienced* where all that bumping and grinding could get you — although some of the details I was most anxious to know had been left out. It was a wicked thing, she said, and she was glad that Jesus had saved her from it. This pamphlet had apparently escaped my parents' notice, otherwise I knew the pictures wouldn't have stayed on the wall as long as they did.

At my Grandpa's house I heard Pat Boone sing on the little Electrohome radio, *Well-a well-a everybody's gonna have religion in-a glory, everybody's gonna have a wonderful time up there;* and he sang at Speedy Gonzales to come home and get some enchiladas in the icebox; sang about a girl who laughed while he cried when their love letters in the sand were washed away; or sang about the moody river that made my loins ache for the girls who were always just out of reach — or way out of reach.

But then on Grandpa's record player, Pat sang about coming to the garden while the dew was still on the roses; how God walked and talked with him there, and the joy the two of them shared none other had ever known. I knew the hymns well enough, and I wanted to learn a lot more rock 'n' roll; but to have religion in glory, *and* a number one hit-parade tune about it, was something else again — like Pat's good luck in walking with God — whereas I had mostly been watched from heaven, and was pretty sure that God could barely tolerate what he saw.

The *Star Weekly* was an insert in the Saskatoon *StarPhoenix.* We didn't subscribe to the newspaper, but Klassen's Transport brought copies from Saskatoon, and Jacky Unger, who lived next door to my Grandpa's, delivered them around the village. Sometimes on Saturdays if he had any leftover *Stars,* he'd give me one, which was how I acquired the pinups.

Jacky's father was one of the Mennonites who smoked Black Cat cigarettes and played cards, and had married a Presbyterian woman from somewhere else. He often said *by gully*: "It's a nice day, by gully," or "Was that you, by gully, I saw at the gravel pit yesterday?" But even he had his limits: "By gully Jack, you better get your hair cut, or I'll cut 'em off myself."

Still, Jacky's life looked pretty good to me. His hair was nearly as long as Elvis's, he stayed out till ten on Saturday nights, and God only knew what he and the boys did; I was just lucky to have someone like him for a friend.

Sometimes the *Star Weekly* had small black-and-white photos of movie stars along with the full-colour pinups, and one day at Jacky's house I found another picture of Sandra Dee that didn't look quite as pure as the one on my wall. It was small enough to fit in a shirt pocket, and when Jacky gave me that magazine I could hardly believe my good luck. I carried it through his backyard and climbed over the fence into Grandpa's garden, and headed for the cornpatch.

Grandpa had planted a new variety that year, and the stalks grew high over my head. Under the corn's dark foliage I salvaged two things from the *Star*. One was a new picture of Perry Como in his famous two-toned shirt, with the V from collarbone to navel. I tore it out and sang, *Find a wheel . . .* and my heart went round, round, round; and a few pages over it led me to the one I loved — Sandra Dee in a dress with a V that probably didn't mean virgin, although I didn't like to think about the photographer, and what he maybe did with her later. But this was no furtive glance; here was a vision stretching to the end of time, with a V by gully that looked better than Perry's, and in the middle of the cornpatch I said, "Oh Sandra, I love you," and ripped her photo out too. I stole through the neighbour's hayfield to the CNR tracks, and disposed of the *Star*, and held Perry in one hand and fondled Sandra with the other. And realized I couldn't possibly take her home.

I tried to think of a place to hide the picture for when I'd need to refer to it again, and went ruminating back through Grandpa's garden and chicken fence; and when I got to the outhouse, I happened to discover the perfect hiding spot. Up where the wallboard met the rafters there was a tiny warp; and when I climbed up to the seat, that space looked as if it had been made for hiding the very picture I carried in my pocket. I slid Sandra into it so neatly that when I sat down again, she had vanished. I climbed back up to make sure the system worked — retrieved her and hid her again — and went home whistling, and hung Perry up on the wall between Elvis and Debbie Reynolds. And now Sandra's pinup smirked at me; she knew what I knew.

Over the next week I spent a lot of time at Grandpa's, coming to the garden alone, or going to the toilet more often than usual. Sandra Dee went in and out of hiding, and didn't seem to mind. I visited her a dozen times and she was always there, came obligingly from the wall, and went patiently back again. There was a tense moment one day when my cousin Rueben and his dad came from the farm to get grease from North Star Oil, and dropped in to see Grandpa. I had an urge to introduce Sandra to Rueben, and went to the outhouse while he waited, and came out fairly quickly not counting on Grandpa and Uncle Harry noticing. "Hey, city slicker, that was a fast one," Harry said from the workshop door, "you must've not had to go too bad."

I was proud, thinking about it later, how quick I had been replying, "No, I was just blowing my nose, I needed

some toilet paper." Grandpa said blowing was better
than picking, and Rueben grinned as we headed for the
garden, and said, "Boy that was close." I felt smug as he
viewed Sandra. If he was never jealous of me before, by
gully, he was then.

One afternoon Jacky and I went to the junkyard north
of town, and came home along the railway tracks as
usual with new treasures. I had found a ring with a stone
that could easily be a diamond, and Jacky had salvaged
a Lone Ranger pin from a discarded pair of jeans. When
we got to the stockyard across the street from Grandpa's,
Jacky said he had to go and deliver his *Stars*. I rubbed
my diamond ring and thought I might as well look in on
Sandra before going home for supper.

In the workshop I chatted with Grandpa as he planed
some two-by-fours, but quite soon had to go to the toilet.
Inside, I fastened the hook and climbed on the seat. One
tattered corner of Sandra stuck above the wallboard, but
as I grasped at her she vanished, and I heard her slide
down behind the wall and stop six inches below.

"Shit!" I said, and tugged at the wall, and Sandra
slipped down to shoulder height. "Shit, *shit!*" twice like
that — I pulled harder, and now she slid toward my
knees. My face turned hot and hope was dribbling away,
when an idea came to me: why not send her all the way
down and retrieve her at the bottom? I jumped from the
seat and knelt on the floor; tapped at the wall again,
pulled and tapped, and hoped that Grandpa wouldn't
overhear; and sure enough, Sandra went all the way
down.

"Come on now," I said, two left fingers between the
floor and the wallboard, right index-finger prodding.

Just about. "Please, Sandra — *please.*" Left knuckles white from the strain, and I let up a bit, she was *that* close.

Again. Wedging, left hand pulling, lifting, right finger pushing; she was right *there*, "Come *on*, Sandra." Another pull from the left, and one side of the wallboard ripped loose from floor to rafter, and hung with every screw torn through the fibre and six jagged holes gaping at the edge, and now my luck had run out.

I stayed on my knees for a second and grabbed Sandra where she'd fallen, but everything had turned huge. I'd buggered up the toilet and I had to get out, get away. Now the ring didn't look like a diamond, nor the cornpatch a good shelter, and the V wasn't all it was cracked up to be, and already Grandpa was thinking why would someone rip a wall apart except to fetch out a dirty picture? And Pat Boone started singing *Well-a well-a how you gonna feel about the things you'll say on that Judgement Day?*

I had to get to the driveway, from there to the stockyard; and I'd have to get saved all over again, if such a thing were possible. I opened the door and stepped out, tried not to flee, not to look at the workshop. I got as far as the coalshed and turned toward the lane, where the stockyard came into view. And halfway through the yard, in the middle of a giant step forward, I heard Grandpa's anvil chime from the workshop door.

It sounded like the gavel of God.

PLASTIC FLOWER

ONE NIGHT IN 1964 soon after getting my licence, I was taken to task by my minister for driving recklessly on Main Street. He blocked my way down a claustrophobic staircase between the balcony and main floor of the church one Wednesday night after prayer meeting. We teenagers had knelt on a bare floor that sloped down toward the sanctuary, facing the backs of the benches — they could hardly be called pews — and taken turns reciting our petitions: God bless so-and-so missionarying in Peru, such-and-such a couple trying to save Indians around Montreal Lake, every acquaintance in "foreign lands and north lands," as my father divided the world in his prayers at breakfast — bless every one of them. We had entreated God, too, for our wayward relatives in BC and Ontario: "Grant them neither peace nor rest until they return to Thee." The minister had just heard me pray like this, yet he felt constrained to halt my descent to the parking lot, and admonish me.

"I've heard how you squirrelled your tires on Main Street," he accused, nervously twisting a corner of his flappy leather Bible. And how did I think this was a good witness to the many lost souls around us, or consistent with what I'd just prayed up there? His tone was not angry; but if I was squirrelling tires now, who knew if I wouldn't be rocking on city bandstands next, like they were doing in Pittsburgh PA?

And indeed, a few months later, I became a rock star for one night.

By hoarding and scrimping, I had managed to buy a used single-pickup electric guitar with a Harmony amplifier. My friends and I plugged in when our elders weren't listening, and one of us picked out sparse lead guitar while the others added rhythm with rock 'n' roll's four basic chords, and we felt gleeful and wicked at how the girls would love us if they ever heard us play. I had never been on a date, though I'd read books like *Christian Youth and Dating,* that urged going out in groups and offered such advice as: "If you like the hostess's punch, don't ask 'What all have you got in here?' Say rather, 'This surely is a good drink.'"

I first laid eyes on Fay the summer I was seventeen, when she sang in the choir at a missions conference in the neighbouring town where she lived. I fell in love with her on the spot, harder than I'd done with anyone since Jane in the third grade. I bribed "Schmidthouse" Schmidt to give me a little school photo of her — hardly bigger than a postage stamp — which he'd traded for one of his; and I made love to that picture every day until school began in fall. It so happened that I was to take my last two years in Fay's town, since our own school ended at grade ten.

My family, which now included two younger sisters, had moved from the little house in the village, to an acreage just at its edge, where we kept some chickens and cows and far too many pigs. For me, everything to do with farm work was tedious at best, and at worst, nearly insufferable.

When I entered Fay's school, I was on the lookout for ways to gain her attention. She was a grade behind me, and in a separate classroom. Early in the semester, I discovered that each spring the student council staged a talent show. As the year wore on, I seemed to make no progress in drawing any notice from Fay; and when the time neared for the annual show, I volunteered both to be the emcee and to bring a "number", as all kinds of performances were known.

That May evening before the performance, I stood examining myself in the mirror of the school's washroom. I had inherited a white jacket from an older cousin, which I hoped would make me look a bit like Marty Robbins, but I was troubled that it seemed too large, as if I were still waiting to grow into it. Onstage, my guitar was propped against the amplifier, and in the audience sat Margaret Neufeld, a diminutive redhead from grade ten and a classmate of Fay's, ready to accompany me on the piano when our turn came. In the preceding weeks we had rehearsed Floyd Cramer's hit *Last Date* several times, and I believe that Margaret would have excited me terribly if I hadn't been so monogamously in love with Fay.

The star of the show was billed as a certain "Mr. X" someone had heard of, who came from behind Saskatoon (it was said), and the posters in school and around town promised that he'd thrill us with his guitar-playing, if not actually lure us to the city's bandstands. But by the time the show was to start, Mr. X had not arrived. We understood, of course, that rock stars are busy people, and decided meanwhile to get underway with our local acts.

Two girls sang a duet, and I scanned the crowd for Fay. A poem was recited:

'Twas battered and scarred, and the auctioneer
Thought it scarcely worth his while
To waste much time with the old violin,
But he held it up with a smile . . .

I spotted Fay near the back sitting with her best friend Anne. My emcee's duties kept me occupied, and prevented undue nervousness about our own approaching number. And when it did come, Mr. X still hadn't shown up.

Margaret walked forward as I flipped the Harmony's toggle to ON and strapped the guitar to my shoulder. She played Floyd Cramer's introduction, and with the amp on full tremolo I picked out the melody of *Last Date: Dum-dum dumdumdumdum dum-dum* (and Magaret's piano replied, *Dumdumdumdum*). How such a thin performance could have met with the applause that followed was a miracle. The crowd had no idea that Mr. X wasn't waiting in the wings to dazzle them, but they clapped as if they saw that I had played my heart straight out to Fay and — who knew — maybe she loved me too; clapped as if they could hardly resist the temptation to rock their own lives away.

I put the guitar down and called for another poem.

Mr. X, we began to think, must have had a more lucrative engagement elsewhere. And when it came time to fulfill the posters' promise, I could only offer an apology on behalf of the student council.

Someone called out, "Play *Last Date* again!" There was a spattering of handclaps, and yells and whistles followed, and I perceived at once that superstardom was beckoning.

Margaret came to the piano again, her red hair and cheeks glowing like a match to my own fire; and we made that huge crowd love us even more.

And they wanted an encore. We had rehearsed several other tunes, and rejected them in favour of *Last Date*, but with such adoration in the air there was no choice but to play. And we did. And before the curtains were drawn, we reprised *Last Date* yet again, and the show ended with applause that might have turned to standing ovation if anyone in the village had heard of such a thing.

I don't know whether Margaret thought I'd ask her out later. It would only make sense, two stars having ice-cream and reviewing their performance. But Adventist Epp's shop had closed at sundown for the sabbath, and besides, Fay had been clapping along with the rest of the crowd, and I had no more eyes for Margaret that Friday night.

As the auditorium emptied, the boys and I stood outside under a tree. I talked with my cousin Rueben, trying not to sound too cool in my rock 'n' roll delirium, these light-years' distance from Wednesday's benches and the minister's tight stairwell.

Under a nearby tree, a group of girls talked among themselves. Fay and Anne were there, and Margaret was not. I found that Rueben had both his eyes on Anne, and

I was relieved — he had already once stolen away a girl I'd wanted to take out after the school Hallowe'en party.

The night was balmy, but I shivered to the applause of thousands echoing in my ears, and tried to guess what it meant that Fay was glancing at our tree sometimes.

Rueben and I withdrew to discuss strategy. Then we strolled as indifferently as we could toward the girls' tree; yet I was surprised to hear myself ask Fay, "May I take you home?"

She glanced at Anne, and said, "OK." Rueben asked Anne the same, and she said, "Sure."

I had driven to the show in the '52 Chev my parents had acquired from Rueben's when his dad bought a new Biscayne. My old car stood in the darkness across from the school, another hand-me-down cursing me in my poverty, I thought. But Rueben had offered to take his Biscayne, and as I opened its back door for Fay, I prayed that she wouldn't look at my '52. I was an evening star, in the back seat of a shiny red sedan, on a first date — and with *her,* instead of with the smudged photo I carried in my wallet.

Although Rueben's car was new, it had no optional equipment, not even a radio. We drove along Main Street, where I had spun my tires. Drove by the elevators and the curling rink. Did the whole town in about ten minutes. We went by "Schmoodle's" Garage out to the highway, another three minutes; followed the pavement around to the town's other entrance, three minutes more; and took that street back in. We cruised with no particular place to go, but not really the way Chuck Berry meant.

What was left was to take the girls home.

However you add it up, I was in the back seat with Fay for no more than half an hour, every minute consumed with fretting over coolness; watching Rueben's right arm feeling toward Anne's shoulder as he drove, and never getting there; trying to imagine what to do and say, and with no idea how.

The Biscayne pulled up at Fay's house, and she and I walked to her door. She said, "Just a minute," and disappeared into the house.

When she came out again, she was carrying a scented plastic corsage. Without a word, she pinned it to the lapel of my white sportcoat, and it cast such fragrance on the night air that I shivered again — better by far than Marty Robbins's pink carnation.

"Thank you," I said, and touched her arm, and headed back to the car where Rueben was just getting into the front passenger side. He said, "Why don't you drive?" and I only wondered how much beatitude could be endured in one night.

The trip to Anne's farm lasted another five minutes. From the corner of my eye I saw Rueben's left arm touch her left shoulder once, but by then we were at her lane. A moment later he had taken over the steering wheel again, and we drove into the prairie night numbering ourselves among the triumphant.

My parents were asleep when I got home. I hung the jacket in my cardboard wardrobe, drew in the aroma of Fay's flower, and tried to get to sleep.

But sleep came hard.

The next day, being Saturday, was devoted to shit. I waded through slop in the pig barn; the ammoniacal chicken-shit nearly drew tears; I piled cow-shit on the wooden stoneboat — so called because it was also used for clearing rocks from fields — and hauled one load after another out to the pasture with our little Massey-Harris 30 tractor.

When I was finished at home, I drove across Grandpa's garden to his barn, and helped with his chicken-shit, and dragged it back to our pasture too, spreading it around for the wind to share with the village. In the evening I went from barns to bathtub, and straight to my wardrobe to inhale Fay's flower again, taking her scent in deep.

On Sunday we went to church, but I don't recall what the minister said.

Monday morning I patrolled the school to catch sight of Fay. In the hallway I saw at once that something was wrong, but lacked the will to find out what it might be. Tuesday and Wednesday only deepened my conviction. Thursday after four, she stopped me on the staircase as I was leaving for home and the odious barns again.

"You know that flower I gave you?" she said, as if perchance I could have forgotten. I had no clue what was coming, but tried to summon the faded superstar image once more.

"Well, it belongs to Anne. I thought she'd see it when you went to the car, and get it from you."

I had often enough considered the possibility that she'd never go out with me again, but I thought at least I'd have that flower to deodorize the remains of my life.

"Oh, I didn't realize," I said.

"Well, could you bring it back?"

I delivered it the next day in a plastic bag, little white-headed pin still poking through its stem. *Woke up Friday mornin', Lord, and brang that flower back.*

She did go out with me once more, and this time my guitar had nothing to do with it. I had joined the school choir, mainly because Fay was in it, and just before Christmas we sang at a carol festival in a nearby town. Later I drove her home, alone, in the '62 Ford my parents had meanwhile purchased from the school principal. It had no radio either, and there was enough silence in the air for me to figure out that she was being kind for having taken away my flower.

Walking Up *the* Stair

THE MAN WHO WASN'T THERE

As I was walking up the stair, I met a man who wasn't there.
He wasn't there again today. I wish, I wish he'd stay away.

— Hughes Mearns

WHEN I FIRST HEARD NORTHROP FRYE'S MONIKER for his childhood deity, "the Old Bugger in the Sky," I laughed at the dead-on characterization of the god I also grew up with — and at the same time winced, knowing that most of my kin would consider it blasphemous. Frye believed that no one in the western world could be considered educated without having read Shakespeare and the Bible. The "fifteen-minute world" that hatched me (a cousin calls it that for the time it takes to drive through) gave us a bit of Shakespeare and a great deal of Bible, and to this day my tongue is heavily accented by the Authorized King James Version.

I catch myself muttering at the Invisible Man who stopped me from taking what Pam Lawson offered under a full moon at midnight in the water of Pike Lake, when we were nineteen and only the two of us were there. And today the old man can still drown out a robin's trill on an Easter Sunday stroll; for guilt, as Garrison Keillor observes, is the gift that keeps on giving.

In the beginning — and this was the truth, our preachers said, not like myths from African or Indian lands — someone named God created the world, with a man and a woman to live in it. But that first couple disobeyed him and made him angry. They ate his forbidden fruit (there was no biblical evidence to call it an apple), and he expelled them from the Garden of Eden. Since then, every human has been born in sin, and unavoidably repeats the disobedience of Adam and Eve. And because evil must be punished, not overlooked, God is forced by his own holiness to curse everyone, from that original pair to the lastborn soul before the Great Trumpet sounds — along with Earth and the rest of nature too: *Cursed is the ground for thy sake; in sorrow shalt thou eat of it all the days of thy life.*

The Creator made the human race, but he soon destroyed most of it in a wrath at its wickedness, and only reluctantly let it start again with Noah's brood emerging from the ark. And the evangelists told of explorers who had climbed Mount Ararat thousands of years later, and discovered the hulk of a big boat up there — no doubt the ark, just where Scripture says it landed, preserved as a warning to us from the righteous Judge of the world.

Although God regretted so nearly drowning the human race, and had hung out his rainbow as a pledge not to do it again, he later burned Sodom and Gomorrha to the ground for its many sins; and when Lot's wife (the Bible didn't give her a name) looked wistfully at the cities as she fled the holocaust, God turned her into a pillar of salt. The preachers brought reports of a pale, weathered column that could still be seen in a middle-eastern desert — quite possibly the remains of Lot's wife, standing as another warning.

And God commanded Abraham, saying, *Take now thy son Isaac, whom thou lovest, and get thee into the land of Moriah; and offer him there for a burnt offering.* Abraham was prepared to obey; but at the last instant, with the boy already tied on the altar, God relented and allowed him to substitute a ram caught in a nearby thicket. This, the preachers said, prefigured what would happen in the New Testament, when the true Lamb of God would die for the sins of the world on Calvary's cross.

These acts of God were described vividly to us, and others I found in my own nightly Bible readings, which were urged on us as devotional exercises. Thus I learned that the Lord once lay hidden by the roadside to catch Moses, and kill him for not circumcising his son. Only the quick thinking of Zipporah, Moses' wife, saved him: she took a flint-shard from the road and severed the offending foreskin, and touched God with it, so that he left Moses alone and went off appeased.

Once God made a wager with the Devil, that his man Job could not be induced to turn against him. And he won the bet, at the price of making Job's name synonymous with suffering; and when the wretch sat moaning on an ash-heap, covered with boils, God said, *Who is this that darkeneth counsel by words without knowledge? Gird up thy loins like a man; for I will demand of thee, and answer thou me. Hast thou an arm like God? or canst thou thunder with a voice like him?*

And there were endless animal sacrifices that God required — blood smeared on lintels, blood on doorposts . . .

Yet he loved his people too, and loved them so much that in the fullness of time he incarnated himself in his only Son, and on that Son visited what he had considered doing in Isaac's case — sacrificing him to propitiate the divine Justice once and for all.

We heard these things in summer camps and vacation Bible schools and revival meetings; we read them in books and tracts. And the Bible was a sword in the preachers' fists as they told how the sacrificed Son had been raised from death and taken to heaven, from where at any time — perhaps today — the Jesus who was meek and mild at his first advent, and willing to be crucified, would come again. A hole would appear in the sky, and he would come riding down on the clouds, with a corona circling his head and a sickle in his right hand; and the second coming would be a bloodbath such as John saw in the *Book of Revelation*, with blood flowing as deep as the war-horses' bridles. Then sinners would be cast into hell, where for all eternity there is wailing and gnashing of teeth — and if we have no teeth, one evangelist said, teeth will be provided.

How long is eternity? If a bird flew a thousand miles to a mountain, picked up a pebble and carried it back; and flew again and again, each time bringing one small pebble in its beak, by the time the mountain was levelled there and re-built over here, eternity would barely have begun. So long and longer we would burn if we did not believe; for unbelievers — whether *in Afric's dark domain,* or in the village Lutheran church, or even in our own pews — were destined for hell.

Although the sacrifice of Christ would admit us — some of us — to heaven, this world had been disowned by God, and we were charged to keep it at arms' length too, except for our duty to take the good news to the uttermost parts of the earth, to save the heathen from perdition.

Ah, and we were children. We wanted to trust promises of forgiveness, but they were shot through with terror; we tried hard to be joyful, but how could we: *Born in sin, and in sin your mother conceived you. All your righteousnesses are like filthy rags. If you keep the whole law of God but offend in one point, you are guilty of all.*

The Old Man up there and his cohorts here below didn't want us to have an adventure. They scared the bejesus into us, wanted us to set out with slogans, not find sums of our own; and we were infected by old-buggerly self-righteousness, while professing to be saved by the merits of some other blood, some cross not our own. Religion became the problem it professed to cure — estrangement, such estrangement from life.

It makes no difference for us that there *is* no such God. The myth is impervious to the intellect that scorns, and the Old Man is in our genes like a medieval virus.

It's our version of the buggered-up blues.

CONCRETE HEAVENS

*Visionaries never see more directly than through the
symbolism by which they are troubled.*

— Phillip Rieff

IN HIS *ANECDOTAL MEMOIR*, CHARLES TEMPLETON —
former evangelist, politician, journalist, and editor of
Macleans — recounts an experience at Princeton
Seminary, where he had enrolled in quest of a more
liberal faith after severing his professional ties with Billy
Graham.

> One night I went to the golf course rather late. I
> had attended a movie and something in the film
> had set to vibrating an obscure chord in my
> consciousness. Standing with my face to the
> heavens, tears streaming, I heard a dog bark off
> in the distance and, from somewhere, faintly,
> eerily, a baby crying. Suddenly I was caught up in
> a transport. It seemed that the whole of creation
> — trees, flowers, clouds, the skies, the very
> heavens, all of time and space and God Himself
> — was weeping. I knew somehow that they were

weeping for mankind: for our obduracy, our hatreds, our ten thousand cruelties, our love of war and violence. And at the heart of this eternal sorrow I saw the shadow of a cross, with the silhouetted figure on it . . . weeping.

When I became conscious of my surroundings again, I was lying on the wet grass, convulsed by sobs. I had been outside myself and didn't know for how long. Later, I couldn't sleep and trembled as though with a fever at the thought that I had caught a glimpse through the veil.

Templeton had been born into a faith much like mine, but I came one generation later, and with more conspicuous ethnic genes. In my early teens, it was a big excursion to attend a Youth for Christ rally in Saskatoon with my older cousins. This was the organization that Templeton had launched with Billy Graham, though by then he himself had abandoned the movement. Our word for Templeton's defection was *backsliding* — if indeed it was not apostasy. I remember sitting in an uncle's farmhouse one bitterly cold winter Sunday afternoon. As the steam radiators clanked and hissed, we listened to our elders debate what they called "eternal security": If you turned out like Templeton, did it mean you had lost your salvation, or that you had not really been saved in the first place? Either way, though our parents themselves seemed quite safe, Templeton's case served as an admonition to us younger ones not to presume that we were beyond such a fall from grace.

Later, when I became a minister myself, another uncle told me of a meeting he'd attended after the notorious backsliding, where a zealot in the crowd yelled toward the stage, "Mr. Templeton! Do you believe in a concrete heaven?" And Templeton replied, "Well, if you mean a heaven of cement and gravel, no, I don't think so." The audience crowed, while the literalist shrank humiliated back into his seat.

In his *Memoir*, Templeton gives an estimate of his experience on the Princeton golf course

> I learned that what had happened to me was not unusual: it has been a commonplace at various times in the history of the church. More important, I learned that it was of no special significance. Mystical experience has added no insight to our knowledge of God . . . Indeed, the experience is not uniquely religious: the poet Henry Wadsworth Longfellow could go into a transport at will merely by repeating his name aloud.

Yet in his novel *Act of God*, Templeton weaves a story of religious intrigue fraught with moral dilemmas and huge sorrow, and gives his Cardinal Maloney an experience lifted straight from that visionary night in Princeton.

> Before him . . . the whole of creation, weeping. The trees bowed down and weeping. Each petal of every flower, weeping. Every blade of grass, weeping. The clouds and the skies and the very heavens, weeping. All of time and space; all that is and has been and ever will be, weeping. And above and around and through it all, God, weeping. Weeping for man; for his pride, his obduracy, his waywardness, his thousand cruelties, his multitudinous hatreds. And at the

heart of the eternal sorrow, the shadow of a cross and a silhouetted figure, and the face he had just seen . . . weeping.

Has Templeton chosen, then, to re-create a triviality in both his writing and his memoir?

No special significance. If he meant this as a Zen adept, for whom nothing means — or intends — anything else, he would accept the vision when it comes and release it when it goes, like any other experience. Then, for instance, a political or journalistic triumph on this side of the veil would have neither more nor less significance than a vision of the universe weeping on the other; all would be met with Blake's kissing the joy (or sorrow) as it flies. But Templeton's memoir implies that the many this-worldly enterprises into which he was drawn, *do* carry the significance that being "out of himself" did not. He discards the vision along with his evangelical myopia, and seems to settle in a world of "aspiring little creatures on a wayside planet," as Raynor Johnson characterizes our human normality. (And Rilke says, "Journalism is a trade in the midst of time, but writing is an art that looks to eternity.")

I myself cannot believe in a hard reality where humans sacrifice a hundred million of their fellows within fifty years of being "in" themselves; where our species' bi-weekly military budgets equal what it takes to feed, clothe, house, provide basic literacy and health care for everyone on earth for a year; where war-news is followed swiftly by canned laughs and talk shows of the rich and famous who are in — or into — themselves. Vision by proxy, by hierarchy, even by democratic majority, is hardly distinguishable from make-believe.

Without original vision, we are prey to charismatic figures rallying us around theirs; and history repeats itself like a stutter — *ein Volk, ein Fuehrer,* normality worshipping a single idol, though Earth becomes a shop of terrors — unless, truly, this is an illusion to make the out-of-himself-Templeton's God weep.

It may be that there is no concrete in the blue heaven; yet the original vision of a mystic like Redwood-Anderson can see on Earth as it is up there:

As if two shining winds of the Spirit, one inward, one
    outward, careering,
one from the infinite sphere's periphery, one from the
    centre's infinite depth,
inward, and outward, spears and arrows, wing to
    wing flashing and answering,
we two in mid heaven so crashed together — crashed,
    and mingled, and passed through each other,
till my arrows had wounded your sphere's periphery,
    your spears had riddled my soul's abyss,
and we two — God and Man — were made one, yet
    two, in the wild white warfare of love.

To See in a Sacred Manner

But let not revelation by theses be detained.

— Emily Dickinson

WHEN BLACK ELK WAS AN OLD MAN, he recounted a dream he'd had at the age of nine, and said of this experience: "I saw more than I can tell, and I understood more than I saw, for I was seeing in a sacred manner the shapes of all things in the spirit, and the shape of all shapes as they must live together like one being. And I saw that it was holy."

The boy was very ill at the time of his dream; but while those around him feared for his life, he was spirited into a world of wheeling horses and flowering trees, of ceremonial hoops and ritual pipes. And he saw a tepee with a rainbow door, and inside were six grandfathers whom he recognized at once to be the Powers of the world.

When the lad's quaking had subsided, the apparitions began to speak. The sixth grandfather, the spirit of the Earth, had long, white hair, and a wrinkled face with eyes that were deep and dim; yet he seemed vaguely familiar. As the boy stared, the old face began transforming itself backward through time, shedding its years until it reached childhood; and Black Elk saw that it was himself, "with all the years that would be mine at last." And when the spirit had grown old again, it said, "My boy, have courage, for my power shall be yours, and you shall need it."

When the rainbow lodge faded, Black Elk saw in its place only "the tall rock mountain at the center of the world" — known more profanely as Harney Peak in South Dakota's Black Hills. Turning toward the plain, he saw another tepee, his own familiar home, with his parents inside bending over a sick child. That child, too, was himself. He entered the dwelling just as someone said, "The boy is coming to; you had better give him some water."

Not long before my own pastoral vocation came to an end, and before I had read Black Elk, I lay in bed one night in anguish. It seemed inevitable that I would leave both the ministry and a long-troubled marriage. This would be the first divorce on the paternal side of my family, which was crowded with pastors and missionaries and Bible students. That baleful night, the God of my fathers again recited the sins I had committed in my blunderings from the dead centre of Christian fundamentalism; and I could only chant a reply toward the ceiling: *Have mercy, have mercy . . .*

Finally came the blessing of sleep; but within it, a greater mercy was given.

I walked on a country path in the still of the afternoon. Off in the distance, from behind a hillock, the sky began to glow. It was not the sun, but another supernal light rising to bathe the scene at my left, where a boy of three or four played in the sand and waterpools beside the way. The radiance revealed a deep intent on his face as he struggled to make something work, and when he saw me he called out, "Daddy, can you help me with this?"

It was obvious that he would have handled his concern perfectly well if I hadn't happened by, and in the effulgent light I knew that he was only inviting me to play.

I looked more closely, and saw that it was myself. Here I was, and there I was — two selves where there had been but one before. The child played and chattered without a trace of self-consciousness, and the middle-aged man stood in his track, too dumbfounded to reply.

But soon the light began to fade, and with it went the child. When I was alone again on the trail, I loosed a whoop of joy on the country air — and woke in my city bed with euphoria singing in the body I called mine.

It's been said that all philosophy can be distilled into one question: Why is there something, and not nothing?

When astronomy and physics train their gazes far out and deeply inward, they are met with a fathomless void that threatens to dismay skeptic and believer alike. Out into the cosmos, down through atoms and particles, till the last remainders of deity have been scrubbed from the universe — who can wonder that some will shut themselves anachronistically in, rather than suffer such appalling emptiness?

But our researches into how things began in a dim prehistoric genesis, and our speculations over how they may end in a future apocalypse, easily divert us from pondering the given-ness of worlds, which Cirlot says "are only different modes of the spirit." Today we awoke in a given universe; tonight we will vanish in the nothingness of sleep, and reappear in worlds whose presence can be hardly less remarkable than this dimension we inhabit now. Here, our days and daydreams may turn commonplace or hellish; then, unaccountably, we are in a world where glory lights the road, where a spent wretch is still an unsullied child, and divine innocence remains busy at its play. Who can say how things begin and end, or how a mercy within a mercy is given?

And who is the real being: black sheep bleating for shelter in a ravenous night; wanderer on a country trail; or child sprung fresh from nothing? Which one: ailing form in a tepee; lad terrified by a shapeshifting face; or spirit as ancient as the Earth?

This is the marvel, that between the voids at the deepest and farthest reaches of our science, there is this eternal now, the shape of all shapes of one being.

To see it in a sacred manner seems faith, and grace, enough.

THE G-WORD

Today's beliefs are the reversal of yesterday's, both are the
laughingstock of tomorrow.

— Elemire Zolla

AMBROSE BIERCE ONCE DEFINED AN INFIDEL as a scoundrel who is imperfectly reverent of popes, parsons, canons, monks, friars, presbyters, deacons, archdeacons, brahmins, priests, medicine men, nuns, eminences, abbots, curates, diocesans, deans, sub-deans, rural deans, abduls, imams, hierarchs, prophets, gurus, beadles, fakirs, mullahs, chaplains, vicars, prioresses, rabbis, lamas, vergers, dervishes, lectors, rectors, wardens, cardinals, sufis, or pumpums (I've abridged his list, having to come up for air myself).

Paul Tillich, the theologian-philosopher who preferred simply to be called pastor, once said he could speak about God at all only with a sense of sublime embarrassment. He loathed the easy familiarity with which humans are apt to use this G-word — a noun without referent, unlike tree or kumquat — construing God as a being among others (the greatest one of all), and use the term as if it were a proper name, with neither the sublimity nor the embarrassment that Tillich himself felt.

Northrop Frye suggests instead that we consider "God" to be more verb than noun, as a process accomplishing itself. And since this must sound heretical to monotheistic ears, Frye adds that the process is not dead, though indeed it may be entombed in a dead language.

Christianity's Athanasian creed, for instance, establishes three persons of one substance — Father, Son, and Spirit — all of them uncreated, yet with B *born* of A, and C not born but *proceeding* from A; and on the matter of whether C proceeds directly from A, or from A through B, there was such Christian animosity, that in the tenth century orthodox and catholic churches separated, with pope and patriarch excommunicating each other for the glory of one Gword in three persons. And now, at the dawn of the third millennium, the factions still find themselves unable to commune together, and clerics in official robes forbid the laity likewise from just going ahead and doing it — have the bread, taste the wine.

How lively, by contrast, these words of the medieval cobbler Jacob Boehme:

> I saw it as in a great deep in the internal; for I had a thorough view of the Universe, as a complex moving fullness wherein all things are couched and wrapped up.
>
> For the Being of God is like a wheel, wherein many wheels are made one in another, upwards, downwards, crossways, and yet continually turn all of them together. At which indeed, when a man beholds the wheel, he highly marvels, and cannot

at once in its turning learn to conceive and apprehend it. But the more he beholds the wheel the more he learns its form; and the more he learns, the greater longing he has towards the wheel, for he continually sees something that is more and more wonderful, so that a man can neither behold nor learn it enough.

Neither must thou think that God is such a kind of Being as is only in the upper heaven, and that the soul, when it departs from the body, goes aloft many hundred thousand miles off. It needs not do that; it is set in the innermost moving, and there it is with God and in God. The true heaven is everywhere, even in that very place where thou standest and goest.

Behold! that is the true, one, only God out of whom thou art created and in whom thou livest; and when thou beholdest the deep and the stars and the earth, then thou beholdest thy God. Then thou art as God is, who himself is heaven, Earth, stars and the elements.

I have been married — for better, for worse, forever — to Christian religion. Yet we have been a disappointment to each other, and I have been seduced by Buddhism's invitation away from fruitless squabbles about g-words. The human species talks about deities, perhaps, for the reason that it uses upper- and lower-case letters. But if the unpronounceable name still has a god-sized function for me, I know that it needn't be so for others. Then, in hopes of diminishing the world's hostility, and with Meister Eckhart: *I pray God to rid me of God.*

As for my "Christianity", I know mostly that I take up my cross neither willingly nor graciously, and to this again Boehme says:

> It availeth not that thou hast the name of a Christian, salvation doth not consist therein. A heathen and a Turk is as near to God as thou who art under the name of Christ. Thou must go through Christ's whole progress even from his incarnation to his ascension. It is not so slight a thing to be a right true Christian, it is the very hardest thing of all. He that thinks he knows it well, has not yet learnt the first letter of paradise, for no Doctors are to be found in this school, but only learners.

When I was a theology student in the 1960s, my teachers spurned the rising ecumenical movement (the principal called it "ecumania"), and quoted the book of *Jude* in stern King James tones: *Ye should earnestly contend for the faith once delivered to the saints* — pointing out that the Greek text meant *once for all*, not *once upon a time*.

In the past half-century science and technology have taken quantum leaps, yet the world remains caught in its doctrinal toils. I say *God,* you say *Allah;* we say *homoousia,* you *homoiousia;* and homeland security sits tight on the Rock of Ages, or hurls it at others.

But *oikoumene* means to inhabit a house, to be at home in a world. Churches continue their official dialogues — sluggishly, for the world has gone beyond — and want us to rejoice if a saint's dry head-relic is returned from Rome to Armenia after centuries of hostility between the loggerheads.

There is another, more prophetic, impulse among people whose differences stem from ancient times — Aboriginal, Hindu, Buddhist, or Monotheistic. This is a more difficult but also more satisfying form of intercourse. The Dalai Lama believes that the greatest challenge of the twenty-first century is to discover people of other faiths, to feel them no longer as threats to identity but rather as its completion, like finding long-lost cousins and their places.

And beneath the outer world lies the enduring challenge of befriending our subjective depths. *Do I contradict myself?* Walt Whitman asks — and replies: *Very well, then, I contradict myself.* And being a mystic, he transforms the demoniac's cry, *My name is Legion: for we are many,* into a hymn of astonishment, *I am large — I contain multitudes.*

In the other direction lies fundamentalism, which is not so much religion as mindset — mind no longer rooted or growing, but merely rutted and on the go. Billy Graham finds no heavenward path in any non-Christian faith; Charles Templeton mixes concrete here below; and the Vatican's position remains as firm as Luther's *feste Burg:* Christ exists fully only in the Catholic Church.

It may be that heaven is happier at one lost-and-found sheep than over the ninety-nine who stay safe in the fold; but institutions built on Christ's body prefer thousands, or millions together, and circumscribe their domains by words — catholic, orthodox, episcopal, charismatic, even fundamental — words that mean something good if you look them up, but that turn into stay-home words, don't-go words; and heaven's joy recedes as the world pulls us no less forcibly into our own adventures.

But if religions are divided in their dogmatic strains, they are united in the generous-hearted folks and the mystics, who see no reason to delay eating and drinking together as the first and gladdest — rather than last and most grudging — sign of cohabiting one world.

For no doctors are to be found in this school, but only learners.

CARLING'S GOSPEL

ONE SUMMER NIGHT IN THE 1970S, two illicit bottles of Black Label beer made the Bible grow holy for me indeed. I was a young Mennonite minister, green as a peapod and with a few neuroses for good measure, and had just been on vacation in Saskatchewan with my family. When we returned to Manitoba, I left my wife and daughters visiting with relatives in Dauphin, and drove on south alone to our home in Morris. Along the way, I stopped furtively and bought the *verboten* lager; not a case or a six-pack — two bottles, and I meant to have a party.

Late that evening, I drew my curtains against the eyes of the neighbours across the street, who had a reputation for what they knew about people in town, and went to get myself a beer from the fridge. The brand had enticed me mainly for its childhood associations — the ads in *Life* magazine *("Mabel! Black Label!")*, and the empties I'd gathered in the ditch, warm and sweet in the summer sun, to cash in for a penny apiece.

I had borrowed a copy of the *New English Bible* from Dwayne Daku, a minister of another denomination, and was due to return it. On my holidays I'd acquired the soundtrack from *Jonathan Livingston Seagull*, and I took it out now and set it on the turntable, and reclined on the floor between the speakers to listen. During the musical Prologue I began browsing through Daku's Bible, and sipped at the beer, and soon Neil Diamond was invoking a lonely sky; and then the glory-looking day...

I had grown up with the King James Bible, and when I left home I could do much more than recite the names of the sixty-six books in order. I had read through both testaments several times, and was familiar with many sublime passages: *He maketh me to lie down in green pastures; he leadeth me beside the still waters.* Familiar, too, with that Bible's excruciating parts: *This is the law of the sacrifice of peace offerings. If he offer it for a thanksgiving, then he shall offer with it unleavened cakes mingled with oil, and cakes of fine flour, fried.* And branded darkly on my mind were the hard sayings come through the mouths of childhood's revivalists: *If thine eye offend thee, pluck it out: it is better for thee to enter into the kingdom of God with one eye, than having two eyes to be cast into hell fire.*

My post-secondary religion and theology classes had also used the Authorized Version heavily; and when I became a pastor it was as if I were preaching in my native tongue (though I liked to toss in the odd *Koiné* Greek term for an added ring of authority). Now, several years into the ministry, on the last day of vacation and late at night in my own house, I began looking up familiar passages, comparing the modern renderings with old King James's. *The mountains shall run with fresh wine,* the new Amos said, *and every hill shall wave with corn.*

61

In the background Neil Diamond launched into the song, "Be" opening himself like an empty page for an immortal word. In Daku's Bible I read of the ancient *shekinah*, which was said to be the visible presence of the Divine: *Trumpeters and singers joined in unison to sound forth praise, and the house was filled with the cloud of the glory of the Lord. The priests could not continue to minister, for glory filled the house.*

Before long I discovered that the first Black Label was empty. I went to fetch the other one from the kitchen, and laughed that the opener in my hand was called a "church-key". In the living room, I sat on the couch and surveyed the "early-mixed Canadian" décor (as an acquaintance had called our furnishings at a glance); but in the new Bible I read: *You will look round your home and find nothing amiss.* And to me, it seemed that this scripture had been fulfilled.

The Skybird's musical odyssey came to the Anthem, and I was reading from a letter of St. Paul to the Corinthians. In the distance, Diamond's chamber violins and cellos ached with longing. The second beer was half-empty; and there came a choir of angels singing *Sanctus Kyrie, Gloria Holy;* and the strings began rejoicing, and I reached the height of the apostolic appeal — *In Christ's name, we implore you, be reconciled to God!* The words ravaged me in the new translation, and drew a few tears, and I fell in love forever with the sound of the word *implore.*

It was midnight, the brown bottles were empty, and I resolved to have my own new Bible. I knew that a scripture could be inspiring, not merely "inspired"; I had heard a Jewish pop-star make such glorious sounds; and Carling Black Label itself had had a role in the rapture.

The following week I returned the borrowed Bible to the good Reverend, and drove to Winnipeg and ordered my own copy from the United Church Book House. I chose an Oxford Study Edition in a bright blue softcover binding. Its front had a mandala of freshest green foliage; the non-canonical *Apocrypha* were included between old and new testaments; and on the back cover was a long list of contributing scholars, with not a fundamentalist or a Mennonite among them.

When the Bible arrived some weeks later, I fondled it as if in sexual shyness, but it seemed to want to open.

Thirty years later, the blue Book is worn and faded from long use. It became my scripture of choice for the rest of my ministerial career. The mandala on the front is crinkled with age now; and on the back, most of the scholars' names have been rubbed away. I fan through its 1600 pages, and stop randomly at passages I once underlined. Some of them I had marked in reverence, some in aesthetic delight, and a few in scorn — my exclamation points jabbing the margins — at how naïve they sounded, even then, to naïve me.

Because I have been retarded by fundamentalist literalism in a world with more Shakespeare than Bible, I've wanted belatedly to catch up with literary pleasures I had never known. I see how easily language becomes an old testament, and how new testaments themselves want to be made newer.

Years ago I set out to re-read the *New English Bible* with, I hoped, fresh eyes, but my progress has involved many sidetracks and delays. Once, the Study Edition languished so long at the back of my night stand, that when I re-opened it at the Major Prophets, a forgotten scrap of a bookmark fell out.

On it were the awkward letterings of my firstborn child when she was just learning her cursive script. *Hellow,* she greeted her Daddy — and she'd crossed out the *w.*

And I could not continue to read, for glory filled the house.

Balaam's Ass

SOME FRIENDS WHO HAD BEEN RAISED in a fundamentalist sect much like mine, also grew tired of traipsing up the aisles for evangelists, and had finally converted to Ukrainian Catholicism. This was an inadvertent return to the faith of two of their great-grandparents; but I was intrigued to visit this new church and watch a baptism, for instance, with priests "spitting" in the children's faces to expel the devil before christening them; and later, when the children could walk, to see them go up this new aisle to "tith de icon" — kiss the icon, as the youngest one said.

In our coffee discussions, it seemed to me that the parents had remained as dogged as ever in their beliefs, only they had transferred their loyalty to a new authority. After some years of lively combat, we reached a tacit agreement to stop debating our religious ideas, but one day we got caught anyway in a discussion of the biblical story of Balaam's ass.

According to the twenty-second chapter of *Numbers*, the prophet Balaam beat his donkey because she kept veering off the road — into the ditch and field, down a vineyard path; and finally at a narrow spot crowded against a stone wall and crushed Balaam's foot. The ass saw an angel standing in the way, but Balaam flogged the beast until she collapsed under him, and (by the King James account) complained bitterly to her master: *What have I done unto thee, that thou hast smitten me these three times?*

Balaam exploded in rage: *Because thou hast mocked me: I would there were a sword in mine hand, for now would I kill thee.*

But the animal asked: *Am not I thine ass, upon which thou hast ridden ever since I was thine unto this day? was I ever wont to do so unto thee?*

Then Balaam's eyes were opened, the tale says, and he was mighty sorry; for there with a real sword in hand stood the angel, who also spoke to Balaam: *Unless the ass had turned from me, surely now also I had slain thee, and saved her alive.*

My converted friend said he believed that the donkey had spoken in human language — no doubt God was capable of performing such a miracle. I asked him then about the serpent in the Garden of Eden; he said it likewise had talked in human words, as reported in the book of *Genesis*. By now I'd taken the bait, and inquired further whether Coyote the trickster also had conversed with Plains Indians in their tongue; but he said no, these were only myths, like fairy tales — and we know the wolf didn't literally speak to Red Riding Hood.

After we had untangled ourselves from this parley, I was very glad that animals had not stopped talking in ancient times; glad, too, that my own ass was not the only one that spoke.

For I often listen to the crow-people: to their rapid-fire *Aw-aw-aw!* their singular leisurely *Awwwwh,* or the interrogative *Awe-awe?* Sometimes I'm sure they're parodying us humans: *Food! Money! Sex! (Smoke?) Workworkwork, moneymoney.* I may be as slow as Balaam to comprehend, and one day a corvid overhead nearly defecated on me to help me past my ego's drivel.

But most often I remember the bear who visited me before daybreak on the Sunday of my ordination in the Mennonite Church. In the dream I was on a road near an old religious college, walking just outside the town limits. A girlfriend from adolescence, grown now to womanhood, passed by me in her car, and stopped farther along the road and talked with two of my old rivals instead. They all looked at me and laughed.

I turned onto a downhill path, and in a secluded place sat in the lee of the riverbank. A cast-iron pipe protruded from the hill, dripping rusty tears that seeped back underground.

Suddenly a huge old bear sat on his rump beside me, looking sideways down his snout as I reached up to stroke his face, and I said sadly, "Things aren't the way they used to be."

He chuckled and replied, "Oh my, no!" — much gentler than the humans above, and speaking so decently that as I woke up, my fears of ordination began to seem bearable (if you can bear the pun) — but oh, his size frightened me, put my poor humanity in its place.

And it turns out, after enough years of dispute with my fundamentally catholic friends, that I myself am a talking animal.

Shepherd, your sheep went far.
Now fold-bound on your back I ride,
eyeing there inside the white woolly ones;
and I, your black sheep with mangled ears,
and burrs in my wool, and one blind eye,
am glad to see them.
When you found me on the ledge
and stretched out a crook to haul me up,
muttering you son of a gun will you never learn,
you gave yourself away — in your voice I heard
that already you'd found an excuse
to give a party.

THREE CHURCHES

Our era has not yet found a suitable cloak for the numinous. It either lays bare the secret or veils it beyond recognition.
— Jolande Jacobi

LONDON

We pause at the doors of Westminster Abbey, visitors from a flat land abased by the staunch towers, seeking refuge from the scurry and fumes of the London traffic. Inside the portal, a small wooden chest at our right greets us with a sign soliciting gifts for the upkeep of the edifice. At the beginning of our first European trip we feel expansive, and donate several English pounds. But then a few steps in, we find that to visit surrounding chapels, or see the tombs of old monarchs, we will have to pay admission; and though we feel less generous now, we pay anyway to go farther inside.

Beyond the prohibiting gates, the sacred house mills with tourists. We scarcely think of ourselves as *them* as we move through the press and into the bowels of the sanctuary. There is the spot where the Archbishop of

Canterbury raised the crown and lowered it on Elizabeth's head. There is the legendary "pillow stone" under the coronation chair, claimed as the rock on which old Jacob slept and dreamt of angels going between Earth and heaven. And we do enter many side-chapels with their overwrought kingly memorials, and everywhere there is congestion. Even at the crypts the curious throng, their cameras flashing weakly under the gloom of the arches far overhead.

Occasionally a public address system pierces the clamour and summons us to a moment of silence. The Abbey pauses, the Lord's Prayer is appended, then the din of commerce resumes. I think of the money-changing racket that drove Christ to take a whip to the temple-traffic of his day, and try to listen inwardly for Rudolf Otto's *Numen* — that which attracts irresistibly, and at the same time makes us shudder. This church would evoke it now if I were alone, at night, among the dead, some of whom have lain here for a thousand years. For when the world sleeps, who knows what spirits under the stones grow restless, or what can materialize at the transept in the high vault above?

STEINBACH

At the Mennonite Village Museum, there is a replica of a church of my ancestors, the sixteenth-century Anabaptists. This worship-house is built entirely of planks — roof, walls, floor, benches and pulpit alike, all constructed of the same rough-hewn timber, and stark as the prairie itself.

The first Anabaptists espoused the separation of church and state as a religious axiom. This earned them damnation from officials who presided over malignant unions of religion and politics, ready always to cleanse the world of heretics. Most of the early Anabaptists were martyred; and of the survivors, many eventually left Europe with its 1500 years of "Christian" history, and went looking for a place of peace. Some came to the Canadian prairies, and the Mennonite Museum has replicas, too, of the sod-roofed hovels where our pioneers lived underground, in a squalour as inconceivable as the ostentations of those medieval rulers.

When they settled on the frontier, the Anabaptists' motto was *Bible and Plow*. Alongside the scriptures, their *Martyrs' Mirror* was a sacred reminder of the forebears who had been killed in the name of Jesus, by Christians. Mennonite ministers were elected by the church membership itself, and they were often fellow-farmers with little or no formal education. They were not, at any rate, men in brocaded vestments chanting Latin texts beneath gilded crucifixes, or locking consecrated wafers away from the people's hands. Their profession was *nachfolgen Christi* — to follow the Christ who would rather be a sacrificial lamb than a high priest.

But if the Mennonite church is austere by day, at night it is desolate. No candle burns before a tabernacled host; no maternal image stretches out her welcoming hands. The world is medievally dark, and the churchhouse proves it — *If heaven's not my home, O Lord what will I do?*

TIEFENCASTEL

A small sign on the Swiss *Autobahn* displays only the generic emblem of a spired church, and we nearly miss it though we've been looking for it. We park at a wayside *Gasthaus*, and walk through the alpine trees on a path winding far down from the highway, toward a river and a secluded place called Muestail. This church is one of only two *Karolingische Dreiapsidenkirchen* built by an order of nuns in the eighth century, and so named for their three distinguishing apses.

At this little shrine, it seems everything must wait forever. A farmer living nearby is hired by the canton as overseer; otherwise, we are the only ones here to enter the gate in the low stone fence that circles the church like a sheepfold. The shingles on the structure are brown and curled, and at places the masonry has crumbled away.

Inside the stone walls the simplicity is shocking. A few wooden benches on the granite floor may once have seated fifty people. The paintings on the walls are faded, their images of almost childlike innocence. Beside the stone altar, a tabernacle is carved deep in one side of the central apse, and secured with the big iron padlock of childhood. A frail cloth in the tabernacle window looks as ancient as the church itself.

This is a silent house. We pause in the centre of the floor. *There is no joy but calm.*

When we turn toward the door again and step outside, evening is advancing. We still haven't looked inside the porch annexed to one wall of the church, and go around to peer through its recessed bars into the darkling interior.

We make out three columns of neatly-stacked human bones, their skulls resting above them, hollow sockets staring out at our eyes looking in. And we can just decipher the sign propped against the central skull: *Was du bist, waren wir; was wir sind, wirst du werden.*

I translate for Larraine: *What you are, we were; what we are, you will be.*

Alone in the dark, I'd shudder here too.

An Improbable Sunshine

CARL JUNG COINED THE TERM "SYNCHRONICITY" (and later referred to it as "a term for which I am to blame") after long discussions with his friends Albert Einstein, Niels Bohr, and Wolfgang Pauli. The concept has been extolled as profound, vilified as sloppy and "mystical", or quietly ignored as an embarrassment to psychological science.

It's not a difficult word to understand. Jung described it as a coincidence of causally unrelated events which have a similar meaning. Suppose one night you dream of a long-forgotten childhood acquaintance, and next morning she phones you from the other end of the world. You catch yourself doing something playful, something you'd long ago become too busy to do, and a sudden freshness pervades the quotidian round. Or you have a day like Hermann Hesse's: the devil spits in your soup, all colours are faded, all strings are out of tune. You push on, supplicating the world to send help from somewhere, and a butterfly lights on your shoulder. You see how a lowly worm has become a

winged, ethereal creature, and there is a small gleam in
the world again.

You don't say the dream *caused* your old friend to
remember you, or that your pleading caused the
butterfly to come; but neither can you deny the weird,
auspicious sense that's overtaken you. Such experiences
have meaningful, not causal, connections. Synchronicity,
Jung said, is an "acausal connecting principle" where
things come together instead of falling farther apart, and
this fusion is a re-birth of energy.

You are skeptical, to be sure, and your mind fills with
scientific echoes — *Random!* — but then Vladimir Holan
replies,

Science can only rummage after the truth:
by inches, not wings!
And I have had enough of your impudence
which thrusts into everything it wants to possess,
and yet does not know how to embrace.

Workaday science concerns itself — competently
enough — with facts occurring within established limits
of probability, typically about 95%. Synchronistic experiences are no less factual, but they sneak up and astonish
us with their *im*probability.

After the throttling of energy I had known in fundamentalism; and later on, dispirited by the kind of
psychology Gordon Allport accused of fixation with rats,
machines, and infants; I was overjoyed to discover
Jung's work. Ironically, it was a religious studies, not
psychology, professor who introduced me to it. And
when its full scope began to dawn on me, it redeemed
both religion and psychology, first with an incentive to

let all their troubled literalisms die, then by reanimating the symbolic powers that had informed both pursuits at their origins.

For years I felt indebted to Jung, and wanted to visit his places in Switzerland for myself. As his work helped to deepen an awareness of my own psychic necessity, my appetite for freedom grew voracious, almost as great as my need for tenured professional work.

Then one night I had a dream.

Four pictures hang in a corner of a gallery — two on one wall, two on the other — sculpted from stone, painted, and chiselled with Latin inscriptions. They are the works of Carl Jung, and each contains a symbol for one of the four medieval elements of earth, air, fire, and water.

I view the exhibit from various angles and distances, recalling Jung's love of stone as a creative medium, and his passion for medieval alchemy. I recall too his encounter with the archetypal anima *described in his autobiography, where a woman tried to convince him that he was an artist. Though the idea tempted him, he resisted strenuously, considering himself to be foremost a medical scientist. Yet here his sculpture-paintings hang in the gallery, clearly regarded as artworks.*

The door opens and a rectangle of sunlight illumines the display in the far corner, and Jung himself enters. He closes the door behind him, and the work hangs again in the gallery's subdued light.

Though Jung is an old man, he walks tall. He doesn't notice me as he approaches the corner, and stands contemplating his creations. At length he mutters, "They're just me, *and I don't care how they're categorized."*

I woke from the dream singing (as the famed "unconscious" arranges things) a tune from the sixties: *Make your own kind of music,* it urged — and do so whether or not anyone else sings along. And later at the kitchen sink, rinsing the coffee pot, I pondered Jung's saying that it's a noble thing to pattern a life after Christ's, but nobler still to live one's own life as truly as He lived his.

This dream had a profound acausal impact. I had wrestled with a fantasy of writing; but was I daft to consider leaving secure employment for a freelance life? The decade I'd spent as a minister had ended simultaneously with domestic separation. For another fifteen years I had worked as a psychological counsellor, trying to stay afloat on the endless stream of others' problems, some of which I shared myself. I met Larraine during that time, and on our first date warned her that I had hopes of becoming a writer. She saw no reason, economic or otherwise, for not exploring a relationship, and three years later we were married.

The work eventually drained me, and I struggled with institutional compromises while clinging to the financial security the position offered. The last winter threatened to make me ill if I stayed much longer in a place my heart had left. Each day the sun struggled from one horizon to the other; every dark night came too soon. And in the back of my mind, Joseph Campbell urged: *Follow your bliss.* It seemed my life had been chequered enough; my parents, I was sure, must be sad that their middle-aged son couldn't hold down a job, and my daughters that their papa was such an incorrigible rolling stone.

On one of the winter's coldest nights, my mentor's work came displayed in four-fold archetypal completeness ("What Freud did for sex," an old joke goes, "Jung did for the number four"). Whether it's art, psychology, or religion; whether inspired by *anima*, by muse, or by spirit; his work, Jung says, is what he is. Other people's rules pertain to their own games.

Soon afterwards I drafted a letter of resignation. I didn't submit it for some months, but writing it felt like an exorcism. And though I didn't recognise it at the time, the synchronous principle was already at work.

Our friend Brent Henderson was employed by a national airline. Several weeks before I left my profession, his company began issuing its workers two annual complimentary passes to be given out at their discretion. Brent promised his first passes to Larraine and me, which is how we came to be in Switzerland ten days after I left my tenured psychological career, as I had earlier left the ministry.

We spent the first day in Zurich recovering from jetlag, and another day exploring the city: the Zwinglian gloom of *Grossmuenster Kirche;* the Swiss-made watches in the shop windows, priced wildly beyond our means; a band playing Dixieland near the *Hauptbahnhof.*

But I was anxious to take the pilgrimage for which I'd wanted to come. The third morning dawned wet and dreary, but I telephoned the C. G. Jung Institute in Kusnacht, a suburb a few kilometres from the city. The receptionist said we were welcome to come and visit. We drove out on the rainy highway, and in Kusnacht stopped at a service station to ask for directions to

Hornwegstrasse. We learned that it was a small street beside the *Zurichsee,* and that we could not drive on it; we would have to park elsewhere and walk to the Institute.

The *Strasse* was indeed a narrow lane bordered by trees and wrought-iron fences, and eventually we came to an old house beside a rather unkempt garden of shrubs and flowers. A small bronze plaque on the gate was inscribed *Institut C G Jung.*

I was nervous when we entered, and we introduced ourselves as the Canadian visitors who had called earlier. The secretary smiled and sounded apologetic in her impeccable English, "As you can see, our place is not very big."

The office was a bright, cluttered room. In one corner stood a bookshelf about the size of one of my own, constituting the English half of their "bookstore". The German half stood along the opposite wall. But the main floor was dominated by an elegant lecture theatre resembling a miniature Adam Ballroom in Saskatoon's Bessborough Hotel. The library on the second floor was bigger than mine, but by an unexpectedly small margin, seeing that many of its holdings were German, French, and English editions of the same books. A few women were there doing research, one very old one among them who looked up and smiled. The third floor dormitory rooms had been vacated for summer holidays. And in the basement, also empty of humans, a few of Jung's paintings lined the walls of the student lounge — disappointing, perhaps, in not being the perfect stone-works of the dream. I was the only male in the place, and I pondered the ways Jung had undermined his patriarchs

— his father who was a Reformed pastor, and the redoubtable Sigmund Freud. I recalled, too, how most of his earliest students had been women. The building hardly felt like an academy; inside, it was just the stately old house it had been from the lane.

We returned to the office and asked for directions to Jung's house and cemetery, and to the tower he had built in Bollingen, where he vacationed often and spent much time in his declining years. The secretary gave us a map. If we saw a red car parked on the property, it meant the family was there and would not want to be disturbed; otherwise we were free to look around as we pleased.

We set out again through intermittent rain, past the family residence where Jung's son, an architect, still lived, to the Reformed Church where I hoped to pay respects at Jung's grave. The cemetery was not in sight, and my facility with the German language too uncertain for me to realize that the *Friedhof* sign was pointing toward it; so we went to the church office for help.

A woman at a copy machine listened to my halting request — *Ich suche C G Jungs Grab* — and went to ask someone in a back room, who directed us to the *Gemeinde* office across the street. The receptionist sent us upstairs to someone else, who had to ask another official, who said that Herr Bierer, the *Friedhof* caretaker, would help us. I began to think that Jung had been forgotten here.

We found the caretaker to be an affable old fellow who chatted pleasantries while escorting us to the family plot. Other people had recently asked about the *Grab,* he said — it seemed unusual. The sun broke through a cloud and cast our shadows before us, and Herr Bierer stopped and pointed at a simple tombstone beneath which six Jungs were interred. And he went back to his work.

My emotions were calm as I stood for a moment with hands folded in front of me. Larraine took a picture, which our friends say looks as if I'm urinating on Jung's grave.

But when we drove away toward Bollingen, I suddenly felt sad, and tried to tell Larraine, who had been raised Catholic, that without this man and a handful of others, I could imagine having disposed entirely of both religion and psychology; tried to say how, with their help, the world has been re-sacralized. But the words seemed feeble.

Bollingen was an astonishingly small village. Jung's stone tower on the *Obersee,* like his Kusnacht school, was inaccessible to public vehicles. We parked at the train station and approached an elderly gentleman from the village. Yes, he said, he had seen Jung's tower once. He scratched his head and tried to remember, and finally pointed us along a footpath beside the railway track. We had walked for some minutes when suddenly there was a great shouting behind us. The old man waved for us to come back. He had checked with someone in the restaurant, and he had misinformed us; we had to go the other way. And he added what the Institute's secretary had already mentioned, that the tower is so concealed among trees that it's easy to miss. We thanked him and started over.

We walked for half an hour, inspecting each place carefully, so we thought. We sat on a bench beside the track and ate our sandwiches, and walked on. Eventually we came upon a young man cutting hay with a scythe in his pasture. I began asking, *Koennt ihr uns sagen wo C G Jungs . . .* but he broke in and finished for me . . . *Jungs Turm, ja, ja.* Many people ask about the tower, he said, and directed us back along the path. We had missed it after all.

Alas, the red car was there.

Then I endured one of my life's strongest temptations, and considered sneaking in through the trees at the back of the property, where the lake began. Larraine wondered how *we* would feel at having our privacy so invaded, and her good sense finally prevailed. We returned to our car and drove regretfully back to Zurich's *Altstadt*, and had a bad but nonetheless expensive dinner.

Dusk was closing in as we arrived at our room, and the rain was falling again. Except for a brief moment, it had been gloomy and wet all day. It was when Herr Bierer led us to Jung's resting-place, and I stood in that comically reverent pose, that the sun beamed on the *Friedhof;* and it had withdrawn again behind the clouds when we left, and stayed there.

The Jungian analyst Edward Whitmont describes synchronicity as the experience of external events beyond our volition coinciding with unconscious inner trends striving for expression.

Winter has returned in Saskatoon, and the weather is not too hospitable now, though on some days the light can dazzle the snow. But one summer afternoon in a cemetery in Kusnacht, it happened that a long-desired pilgrimage was lit by an unlikely burst of sun. And something shines in this prairie winter, if not from the outer skies then from within a rejuvenated soul. When a great man's science helps to realize this, it can also be called art — or spirit, or what you will.

There was another dream on one of our first nights back in Canada.

Larraine and I are in Kusnacht, looking through the front yard of Jung's house, where a flower garden is bordered with stones carved in the shapes of other flowers. Jung's son who lives there comes to greet us, and invites us in to meet the family. He says that he and his brother grew up in this house, and that their father was a psychologist. I try in my floundering German to say that I've been deeply moved by his father's work, but the words don't come out well, and I can only say simply, "Vielen Dank."

Now his brother, also an old man, comes to welcome us just as affably. We follow the pair into the house. Many family members have gathered, and it's fine with them that we're there.

Heartfelt thanks. *Vielen Dank.*

MAKING PEACE

ONE WEEK IN EARLY DECEMBER, the lone Native student in Adolescent Psychology came privately before our night class to say that she was unhappy with her small group. She and four other women had been working on a project, and as far as she was concerned, it was not going well. Although this was her last term before graduating with a teaching degree, she was considering dropping out of the course altogether.

I asked her to consider staying, and promised to help if I possibly could. But she doubted that anything could be done. The problem was partly her own shyness, she said, and partly it was the white women's awkwardness toward her. She thought she'd be better off with her own people in ITEP, the Indian Teacher Education Program down the hall, even if it meant missing the next convocation. When our talk ended, I was quite sure I'd never see her again.

Some time later when the projects were complete, the four other women from that group came one night in a testy frame of mind at the low mark they'd received on their work. They hovered at the front while other students packed their bags, and I noticed from the corner of my eye that the Cree woman — who had stayed with us after all — was about to slip through the door. I called her back and asked the five of them to wait, and encouraged the stragglers in the room to vamoose.

When we had privacy, I summarized the issues. "Four of you are upset with me about the grade; one is unhappy because she feels ostracized by the others. Can we settle in, and see what we know about peace-making?"

For the first quarter of an hour, the four women took turns asserting that they had done everything required of them — it was not their problem. The Native woman accused them of rejecting her contributions early on. She had wanted to address the special ways that Aboriginal children were at risk, but they'd dismissed her ideas and forged ahead with their own. They retorted that their intentions had been good — they didn't want to single out any one group for fear of seeming racist. Everyone's words bristled.

Just when I feared the exchange would end badly, there was a lull, and one of the four women began to cry. She apologized for having been absent so often. Her first baby had arrived midway through the semester, and sometimes she had missed classes for that reason. But now she wanted to say something she'd never told anyone except her husband before: that she suffered from depression, and so severely that she had attempted suicide half a dozen times; and she, of all people, could have had her eyes open for someone else who felt excluded.

Then another woman who had often been strident and brusque, said that she also had been rejected as a child; being Greek, she was often teased for her olive skin and black hair, and she too might have taken time to remember what it felt like — she wasn't exactly a "white person" herself.

A middle-aged woman with a deeply-pocked face spoke up, and acknowledged in tears that she hadn't either done enough to strengthen ties among the group. And finally, the woman who'd been first to insist she had done everything expected of her, recanted; and in a quavering voice she said, "I'm so sorry, sorry I didn't do more . . . "

By now the Cree woman was wiping her own tears, and with eyes averted in her people's way of showing respect said, "I was angry. But now the anger is gone. I never thought it was all your fault. I didn't do as much as I could have either."

There was a silence. I broke it only to say that I had worried about seeming an insensitive masculine lout, or another prejudiced white guy (though I noted that we ethnic Mennonites are actually kind of pink), and my eyes were not dry either.

I thanked the group for their early Christmas gift, and offered one in return. I raised their grades to a B+, but inwardly wanted to defy university regulations, and enter on the Registrar's triplicate form the full hundred percent they should have had.

Later, I followed the river on my drive home, and among the lights and nativity scenes of the opulent houses on Saskatchewan Crescent I recalled another Indian girl I'd known. Somewhere among my treasures was a paragraph written by a grade three student named Alice Starblanket. When I got home, I searched for it and read it over once more.

"In my reserve," Alice said, "you can do lots of things. But my great-grandmother had to kill bears for my mom's clothes. Mom showed me those clothes. So that's how she was born. But I was born in Saskatoon in St. Paul's Hospital. It's fun too, but I wish I was born in my reserve. But I am glad I am born no matter where I was born, just as long as I was born."

A wassail, I thought, for nativity.

THE SALVATION OF HARVEY NICOTINE

HARVEY NICOTINE WAS IN TROUBLE because he didn't want to attend Mass. The vice-principal had heard him out and said he'd be allowed to skip this time, but would have to undergo counselling for his problem, and would be expected at Mass next time, as usual.

Harvey came to my office and repeated his story. A terrible thing had happened at his reserve during the summer holidays, just shortly after his fourteenth birthday. He'd been out riding his bicycle near a large pasture, when he saw two men in a far corner standing over the carcass of a cow. It made him curious, and he left his bike in the ditch and headed over to see what had happened. But as he arrived, the men whirled around, and he saw inverted crosses on their foreheads and cultish emblems on their clothes. He was terrified — he knew they had just sacrificed this animal and he'd caught them by surprise; and they seized him and threw him headlong onto the body, and as he fell, he passed out.

When he came to again, the men had vanished. He leaped from the cow, saw that he was covered from arms to pantlegs in blood, and took off in panic for his bicycle, and pedalled home to clean up. And from there went straight to the reserve church to pray.

As he entered the building, he was suddenly over-whelmed by nausea, and nearly threw up. He hurried outside again, and when the waves subsided he went back into the church, and again nearly vomited and had to leave. He had tested this back and forth several times, until he knew for certain that the men with the ominous crosses had hexed him to be sick when he went to church. And that, he said, was why he couldn't attend Mass any longer.

Harvey and I had known each other for most of an academic year. He had told me many egregious drinking stories during this time, and himself thought that he might have a touch of the Fetal Alcohol Syndrome his teachers talked about. I knew he would not be offended when I asked, "Were you drinking this time, Harvey?" But he said vehemently, "No! I'm telling you the sober truth!"

I wondered about the administrative notion of therapy as tune-ups to make kids function right (and have it done by next Mass), as well as at the plausibility of Harvey's tale itself, but instead asked, "What would it take for you to know for sure that the curse was broken?"

He replied at once, "If I could only walk into a church without wanting to puke, and sit and say a prayer, I would know I was OK."

I promised to stick with him till the issue had been resolved to his stomach's satisfaction, and privately recalled Reinhold Niebuhr's sentiment that the church is like Noah's ark: you couldn't stand the stench inside if it weren't for the storm outside.

After about a dozen meetings, we had contrived a plan that Harvey was to carry out any time he felt ready. I would take him to St. Frances — a church he knew from having attended their school's "social adjustment class" — and there he would do the following things: breathe consciously and relax before going inside; remind himself that no cow-cult had more power than the Creator; enter the church slowly and monitor his gut as he went; back off the instant nausea threatened; relax, breathe, and repeat further; and so on until he could get to a pew and say his prayer.

When the day came, we parked at the front door of St. Frances and reviewed the procedure once more. I asked him, "Is there any special prayer you'd like to say?"

He pondered a while, then began to recite a childhood verse I had known myself: "Now I lay me down to sleep . . . " but his voice trailed off, and he seemed embarrassed that he couldn't remember any others.

"I think that's a good one, Harvey," I assured him; "many people say it when they go to bed, hoping God will look after them while they sleep." I asked whether he'd like me to accompany him, but he said he preferred to go alone.

"Then I'll wait here and say a prayer too, while you're in there."

I watched the Thunderbird crest sewn on the back of his jacket go through the door and fade to a shadow in the foyer. And in my own manner, I did pray.

Within two minutes Harvey was back in the passenger seat, looking straight ahead through the windshield and not saying a word. We sat silently until my curiosity goaded me to ask, "How are you, Harvey?"

"I'm good," he said, and fell quiet again.

After a while I inquired, "Did you say your prayer?"

"Yup."

A long silence.

"Did you feel like vomiting?"

"Nope." Longer silence.

Seeing that he was not offering information, and being unwilling to leave without some inkling of our medicine's effect, I asked him directly: "Well Harvey, how *do* you feel?"

When finally he replied, I barely managed to clamp my laugh.

"I feel saved."

I nearly said hallelujah — but restrained that impulse too. Harvey and I lit up a smoke, and I congratulated him as we drove away from the church.

And here's a late laugh for the Venerable Harvey Nicotine: that salvation of his cut both ways, and was good medicine for me, for sure.

Arul Luthra's Yard

FOR FIFTEEN YEARS AFTER my religious and domestic upheavals, I lived a few steps from the bank of the South Saskatchewan River. My apartment was near the Pioneer Cemetery and Diefenbaker Park, the least developed of the city's parkland, and I could often walk a circuit of five or six kilometres without meeting another human. The riverbank was my sanctuary — its chokecherry bushes, its porcupines and magpies, even an occasional deer within city limits, reminded me of the North Saskatchewan valley that had watered my roots, and was still my favourite place for a getaway.

When I met Larraine, who had been city born-and-bred, she soon observed that I was "a country boy but not a farm boy." She moved in with me later; and when my daughters and sons-in-law began bringing their own kids to visit, the mile of riverbank remained my refuge from the city, and became a playground for our grandchildren as well.

Then the apartment block was sold to a business consortium whose only motive, it seemed, was to impose rent increases and let the building deteriorate.

Larraine and I began looking for new quarters, and at the opposite end of Saskatoon found a townhouse priced within the means of an ESL teacher and a hopeful writer. And when we moved there in the spring of the year, I set out promptly to explore our new neighbourhood.

Everywhere people were raking and watering lawns. Up and down the block, and through the community they toiled at their grass-patches, edging and grooming them to look like all the others on the street. No children rolled or tumbled, no one climbed a tree, no wieners or marshmallows were roasted; nothing doing but the shaping of vegetation and clipping of grass to uniform height, with diagonal lines proving whose lawnmower was steered straightest.

But one day I discovered a house that was barely visible for the dense, wild wonder of its front yard. A forest of spruce and birch and poplar at all stages of growth obscured the dwelling behind it. Birds thrived in the treetops; and in the undergrowth, shaggy grasses were spread among daisies, tiger- and day-lilies, wild roses and flowers whose names I didn't know. And if that wasn't enough, crabapple boughs hung over the sidewalk in front, and over neighbouring manicured lawns on either side.

During the first two years in our new locale I walked by this property many times. It made me nostalgic for the old wilderness at the south end of town. Occasionally a car sat in the driveway, but not once did I see a human inhabitant. Often I paused on the sidewalk to contemplate the ever-new features of this urban wildwood. What eccentric human lived in the house, leading his inscrutable life and leaving nature to hers? One day I was arrested by a miraculous crop of mauve flowers that had risen from the jungle floor, and stood so long beholding them that I began to think the owner must be peering out and thinking *me* an eccentric, if not a psychopath. And coming out of the reverie, I was shocked by a kitten's eyes staring up from under a tangle of grass, apparently having watched the full unfolding of my trance.

Our townhouse was comfortable, and we had many conveniences at hand: corner stores that never closed, a pub with a good menu, gift shops and pharmacies at the mall. And Meewasin Park was a ten-minute walk away, with paved biking trails above the riverbank and rugged paths below.

Yet the traffic was never far off. In certain winds, the wastewater treatment plant assailed us with odours as foul as any the animals had made at my childhood acreage. And on one leisurely amble along the river's edge, there was the spray-painted welcome on a storm-sewer: *FUCK YOU.*

One winter day while crossing a school playground, I saw an elderly woman come from the door of my mystery house. She deposited a bag in the trash-can, and went back inside. I was half disappointed that the thriller taking shape in my mind should turn so commonplace; yet I was glad to know that an elder lived there (if indeed she was the occupant), and I could picture her on a Robert Frost night, sitting in a lamplit room behind the trees of her own acre, concerned with she knew what. And for that matter, she *might* be eccentric: I am what I am and let my nature be.

The following spring on an early-evening stroll, I spied a swarthy man with a rake working at the edges of what I had by now dubbed "the non-monotonous place," and summoned nerve to introduce myself. "I love your yard," I said. It startled him: "Really!"

I said that I hoped he hadn't taken me for a lunatic if he'd ever seen me lingering, and he smiled and extended a hand. "Arul Luthra," he said; "come with me, please." He led me through his garage into the backyard, and began telling me more about his property.

"We have moved to this development twenty years ago," he said, "and each year have planted more and more trees and shrubs."

There were at least twenty varieties of them, and he beamed as he named some for me. He cultivated numerous herbs as well, which he pointed out one by one where he'd sown them haphazardly, and invited me to harvest in summer when they were ready: "You may like some tarragon perhaps — or a few chives for your salad."

High overhead, the body of a duck hung off-kilter in a spruce tree. It was only a stuffed bird that had been left in the basement when Arul and his wife bought the house, and he'd hung it out back for the heck of it — who had ever seen a duck in a treetop? Mainly, he removed dead branches from his yard, but otherwise left the plot to its own devices; and indeed the backyard was almost as untamed as the front, though it did contain a modest clearing where humans might congregate from time to time.

I learned, too, that some folks with tidy lawns didn't care much for Arul's wilderness, and had raised invisible thorn-hedges of their own. I sympathized with him, and passed on an axiom from an urban park designer I knew, who had received it from an old Japanese gardener: *Allow spaces for the mind to play.*

The sun was setting, and I thanked the good neighbour for his cordial welcome. We came back through the garage and shook hands once more at his front door. As I turned on the sidewalk to leave for the comforts of my townhouse, there went a striped tail in the twilight, vanishing in Arul's underbrush.

And I couldn't be quite sure it was a cat's.

WINGS

Spring

Lone goose pipes overhead, silent V comes winging two acres behind. I edge toward a pair of Canada Geese who've settled under a spruce tree near the Forestry Farm parking lot, speaking in low tones to assure them that I come in peace. They're a welcome sight after another hard prairie winter. I'd like to see them closer-up, and they don't seem to object.

I stop for a moment and wait. I imagine their perspective in high flight, how remote from troubles they seem up there in the blue. I tell them that I myself fly sometimes in dreams, and perhaps have a glimmer of what it's like; that one night I sailed up to the spire of a cathedral, and looked over a dark panorama, and far below the lights of the chancery blushed, and two priests went in and shut them off.

I take another step, and wait again. I remember one spring on a muddy path beside the river, hearing the resounding *ke-CHUNK* of a shard of ice breaking and plunging into the water; and a goose that had been resting on it swished with its wings, rose slightly in the air, shifted over two feet and alighted again. I marvelled at the nonchalance. *If you have wings and your bottom falls out, lift and re-settle.*

One more step, another pause. The gander grooms himself. The goose tucks her head down beside her wing. Last year above the riverbank I saw a gaggle of geese on a sandbar. I followed a path down, and sat near them to watch. A narrow channel of water separated us, and I was of no concern to them; but they soon detected the two humans coming through the willows at the far end. The lead goose grunted and slid into the river. Three others followed. Within minutes the whole flotilla was facing the breeze — I love their ascensions — and they rose for me and the world was a wild winging honk-a-lonking, divine moment all full of geese.

Another step. Halfway to the tree now. The gander looks my way, and I linger again.

I have seen geese on the river angling toward a rocky weir on an island, where a hidden brood of goslings waited; and heard how they sat then, trumpeting in the joy of being home. *Behold the fowls of the air,* they navigate wind and watercurrents beyond fathoming, and die without protest into human ears . . .

. . . and suddenly this gander hurtles toward me hissing, and I stumble back, and he's airborne straight for my head; I whirl and bolt, trip on the pavement, rear up and lurch toward the car, peering over my shoulder; the creature lands and stretches his neck like a viper, and my skinned palms and knees begin throbbing, and I see that I've torn a big hole in my jeans.

Yes, a Hindu parable says, God is in the elephant coming toward you — but also in the mahout sitting on the elephant and shouting, *Get out of the way, you dodo!*

Ganderdander, I have learned, is God's voice drawing a line: *So far, buster, and no farther.*

Summer

Today I earned bread by the sweat of my brow. I settle into a recliner and begin meditating to David Hykes's *Hearing Solar Winds,* his harmonic choir making unearthly music in a twelfth-century Cistercian abbey with nothing but their voices. They evoke echoes of the "Big Ring" where Creation comes into being — Hykes refuses to call it a big bang, which he says sounds too much like the noise and violence of our own culture. The solar winds pass through me for an hour, and I begin to feel clean again, and calm, and I sleep a while in the chair.

The sun is near the west horizon when I awake. I go to the patio door to watch the river from my balcony as the sun goes down. With my left foot on the threshold, and right hand opening the screen, a flurry of wingbeats nearly knocks me back into the living room. I've never seen a bird like this in the neighbourhood. It's a dove, and I've frightened her, and I freeze with one foot inside and the other out. She lights again on the rail and folds her wings, and looks at me.

I move with infinite caution until both feet are on the balcony; then, as slowly close the screen behind me, and ease my frame into a deck chair.

Sabbath lasts until sundown. The choir's sounds have stilled me, and it takes only a moment to re-settle. The bird sits at arm's length, facing the river. A few biblical images drift in my mind as I watch: the dove returning to Noah's ark, settling on the captain's outstretched hand with an olive leaf in her beak; the spirit-bird hovering over the Messiah's head as he comes up from the Jordan at his baptism; other fowls of the air who neither sow nor reap nor store in bins, who might therefore inspire us to trust.

I invite the dove to instruct me. She sits.

Will she grant, then, a few of the *ku-kuings* I remember from childhood in my cousins' haylofts in Springfield? No, not that.

I try to remain still, but fifteen minutes is a long time for a busybody to sit. The dove herself does not share this problem. She's feathered steel-grey with a few ebony markings. On her neck, the slanting rays of the evening sun light up delicate pastels — mauves, pinks and greens — and from the one circle turned toward me, I see that her eyes have fiery rims around yellow irises perforated by jet-black pupils. She is content, and I see how little it takes to make her so. *O that I had the wings of a dove to fly away and be at rest!* The psalmist laments, while the dove says *This is how that looks* — instructing me after all, making me smile.

In the end, it's my attempt to show gratitude that drives the teacher away. A half-hour has passed since my arrested step onto the balcony, and it seems I should offer the bird a gesture of thanks: I will feed her. In the kitchen, I pour some rice into the lid of a Mason jar, take it back out, set the offering gingerly on the rail, and ease into the chair once more.

She doesn't seem interested.

I reach over and slide the lid an inch closer. No response.

I try again. No. Closer. Still no answer.

On my fifth try she flies off and out of sight. And for a little while I really do sit still.

Fall

Drab cloud-cover, thin snow blanketing the ground. The wind blurs my vision at once, but I look past the tears, turn up my collar and walk on through the park, to an old pine tree under which I sometimes sit to confess my sins.

I duck under the boughs, stand beside the trunk, crouch at its gruff base for shelter. And suddenly feel an urge to climb. *But I'm over fifty*, the voice of reason objects; *who climbs trees at this age?*

The lowest branches of the canopy are above my head, and I look up, a bemused skeptic, toward the crown. Yet the pine has arranged itself obligingly: there is a way to the top, if I can rise to the occasion.

I recall my grandfather's oak tree among whose upper leaves I indulged in heady boyhood fantasies; I petition for strength to defy my arthritic cricks, scramble up to a low branch, and already don't care who might see me.

The path twists upward like a corkscrew, yet the climb is easier than I'd imagined. Within two minutes I'm perched as high as the tree's steeple will allow, my left arm hooked to a branch as I gaze out at the city.

The top of Saskatoon in late November is a cold place to be.

A gust of wind sways the pine so that it moans, and I clutch at my branch. A fat form whirrs down — "Hel-*low!*" I say, and it turns tail and leaps farther out, and turns again to view this tree-beast from a healthy distance.

I have only one category — bird — for this little visitant. I remember the pictures I once collected from shredded wheat boxes in my childhood — the cardboard dividers between layers of cereal-pillows — and guess *Cedar waxwing*, and resolve to look it up later.

The tiny soul chirps loud, and I chirp back. Or I try. Yet my peeps and whistles sound pathetic even to my ears, and evidently they confuse him a bit too. He hops back and forth; rotates; cheeps toward the city; cocks his head this way, that way. Relocates to a higher branch. Chitters again and audits my replies, bounces vigorously up and down. Then he has other things to do; and when he flies off across the river, I regret that he didn't find me curious enough to stay a bit longer.

Winter

The aperture is small. Smoothness of flow varies with steadiness of focus.

Try to fill the bird-feeder without shaking or spilling.

This little structure is a housewarming gift from our friends. I move it from the kitchen counter into the sink, in case of a mess. Set the plastic bag down, take out a pair of scissors and visualize a clean cut.

I pour, and sunflower seeds bounce on the galvanized metal — *ping, ping* — but this is my first attempt, so I try to relax, keep on pouring, stay aware. Ah! left hand under the bag needs to feel for an optimum flow, and hold still.

My eyes fasten on the waist of the "hourglass" where the seed-current runs strong; and *by yiminy* (said with affection for Peter Gzowski, who said it on *Morningside*) there is rapid improvement: *This student shows good promise; regular practice should raise his grade.*

It looks as if about fifty seeds have spilled in the tub. I scrape a handful together and begin inserting them carefully into the feeder, another chance at non-spilling, right hand shaping a funnel as the seeds flow through.

And I nearly do it. Only a few of them drop beside the base, and one more swipe cleans them up. So rapt have I been that not once did I think about religion, not bad for an old Zen impostor — and *Duesent noche mole eent!* (quick reversion to Mennonitespeak) I knock the bag on the counter and spill a hundred new seeds; they jump to the ground, scamper under the fridge and to remote corners of the kitchen. Now I have another Zen job: to sweep the floor. I fetch a dustpan, and laugh at Armin Wiebe's rendering of the Low German expletive that's slipped out: *Thousand yet once again one!* (Don't ask — I don't know either.)

With all the seeds finally where they belong, I carry the feeder out in the February wind and hang it on a pole next to the hedge. Hasten back inside and hunt for the bird-call my children gave me for Christmas. And from the warmth of my office, open the window and squeak out an invitation for the *angelloi* to come and get it.

The first sparrows and nuthatches arrive. They jitter and peck, and I sit at my desk and plan the day's agenda.

Give us this day our daily seeds.

The Play *of* Forces

THE HEART OF THE MATTER

This is the marvel of the play of forces, that they so serve the
things wherethrough they flow:
growing in roots to dwindle in the tree-trunks, and in the
crowns like resurrection show.

— *Rainer Maria Rilke*

ON A MIDSUMMER EVENING, I pause in the Pioneer
Cemetery at the southern fringe of the city, to rest a while
beside the sleeping colonists. Bees are busy — but sound
drowsy — in a maze of fescue and wild rose bushes
nearby, and across the river a scarlet sun waits to be
tucked under the rim by the Holy Ghost's white feathers.

City traffic frets the avenue on one side of the field;
and on another, a train crosses the trestle on the South
Saskatchewan, and rumbles off toward the east. In this
tract of naked prairie, maintained as an historic site, one
hundred and forty-four souls — a third of them infants
— are buried on the river's brink under the open sky.

They are the founders of the temperance colony that grew to be the city of Saskatoon.

At the heart of the cemetery is a grave with a chokecherry bush on it. I have watched its boughs grow taller each year, until they stand higher than my head; and for the first time I see that new shoots are sprouting on the outside of the headstone. The child lying there is becoming more and more bush; soon he won't be underground at all. City workers have turned his memorial out to face the river, so the inscription can be read.

In Memory Of Vernon Leo
Beloved Child of Mr. & Mrs. J. M. Kuhn
Born November 27, 1902 Died July 19, 1903
Gone But Not Forgotten

I remember one autumn when I was spiritually bereft. After losing a vocation and a marriage (and I feared a family, too), when I saw the chokecherries on Vernon Leo's grave, I wanted to make a wine from them. I picked the ripe fruit one Indian summer afternoon, and was given — I didn't know how — an experience of union beyond religious monopoly, where for an hour I belonged to the world, just as I was and without one plea.

I knew of the cryptic notation that Blaise Pascal had kept sewn into the lining of his coat, and transferred privately whenever he changed clothes, a scrap found only by chance after his death: *Between the hours of half-past ten and half-past twelve: FIRE! God of Abraham, God of Isaac, God of Jacob, not the God of philosophers and scholars!* Although I could not cling to the experience of which this reminded me, neither could I deny the hour "on Earth as it is in heaven," when questions were unasked, and I knew the end — *telos* — of life. The wine I hoped to make from Vernon Leo's chokecherries was intended not for ordinary consumption, but perhaps for some private ritual need.

I mashed the cherries, sprinkled additives at my recipe's instruction, tested with hydrometers, and waited. And eventually siphoned the mix into gallon-jugs, set them on a shelf in a storage room, and waited again for the chemistry to accomplish its work. For two years I rarely disturbed them where they stood beside old boxes of sermons and lectures, and the antique typewriter on which I'd learned the qwerty keyboard in my youth.

One night my friend Guy Giroux came to visit. During the evening, I told him of picking the chokecherries in the cemetery, and of my wish to make a sacramental (if heretical) wine from them. Guy was a devout man, a meticulous teacher of science and an amateur vintner himself (though his friends considered him an expert). I led him to the storage room and pointed at the jugs near the ceiling. He looked closely, cleared his throat to signal his intention to say something, and with typical diplomacy noted several things. First, that my wine had not been bottled and corked; second, that I had let the airlocks on the jugs go quite dry; and finally, that in truth a better place for wine would be a cellar, not a shelf in a warm room. And calling me by a nickname of his own invention he said, "Lloydly, I fear that by now your brew will have turned to vinegar."

I had accepted my failure there and then, and later thought of taking the potion back to Vernon's grave one day, and pouring it out as a libation — dust to dust, vinegar to chokecherry bush. But time went on, and I forgot about it; and too soon after Guy's genteel verdict, he died of a heart attack at the age of fifty-one, on my fifty-fifth birthday.

One mid-July evening I remembered the vinegar on the shelf, and resolved to take it to the cemetery and restore it to its roots. I pulled a chair to my storage room and climbed up to the shelf. There, beside the old cast-iron typewriter (built, I noted, around Vernon Leo's time), were the two gallon-jugs with thick coats of dust clinging to them. I lifted one down and set it on the floor, unscrewed the yellowed plastic airlock, and sniffed warily at the neck.

It didn't smell like vinegar.

I carried it to the kitchen and poured a little into a tumbler, took it out to the balcony, and sat and looked at the river passing below the ground where the pioneers lay. I recalled the two-horned invitations of my childhood ministers: *Come to Christ's table, but beware of eating and drinking to your own damnation.* I recalled visiting churches as an adult, sometimes leaving repulsed by the routine dispensing and swallowing of wafers, so unlike the meal where a man on the eve of death ate and drank with a few wavering friends.

I raised the glass to Vernon Leo Kuhn: *This spirit was to have been your blood; but the vinegar is my own fault.*

At the first sip, I was a guest at a Galilean wedding feast, astounded that the governor should have saved the best wine for last. I was an alchemist baffled by his success. I wished I had been the minstrel Keats — *Thou canst move about, an evident God, and canst oppose to each malignant hour ethereal presence.*

And I knew that, creed or no, I did believe in the communion of friends.

MAIL

WHEN I WAS NINE, I filled out the lines on a cereal boxtop with a Shaeffer fountain pen, sealed the envelope and licked the stamp, and carried my letter to the Laird post office. And began waiting. Two days later the train from Saskatoon came to collect it, and took it to the city where sorters and baggers (I had heard) would put it on the Supercontinental to Toronto. And six or eight weeks later — it seemed a taste of the evangelists' eternity — my coveted Roy Rogers button arrived.

When I was eleven, a mail-order book on kite-making was advertised through the Gem radio on top of our fridge; and I sent off the letter, and waited the long wait again.

At fourteen I contacted a penpal on Cape Breton Island, praying she was the girlfriend I couldn't seem to find in my prairie world; counted days on the calendar, and dreamt of her at night, until her snapshot came, looking more desperate even than I felt.

At eighteen, I spent a day in Springfield's dust, circling forty acres as gulls squawked overhead and splattered me and my Massey-Harris 30; but in the evening I stopped at the post office, and from Box 16 pulled out a fat letter from the Melfort girl I hoped to marry, and went home and closed my bedroom door. This was a letter you could feel.

When the Y2K fever had come and gone, I was barely literate on the computer. One day someone said I needed permission to reproduce a verse-fragment in a piece I was writing: *He thought he saw a Banker's Clerk Descending from the bus, He looked again, and found it was A hippopotamus.* I suspected it was from Chesterton, but hoped to have this confirmed. After days of frustration — phone-calls, hunting through books (who knew from the internet?) — I composed an e-mail offering a beer to anyone who would help. I pressed a key in Saskatoon and the note was gone to a dozen friends. My computer marked the time: 10:51 AM.

At 11:01 AM, Miranda Pearson in Vancouver replied that we live in the age of salvage: go ahead and use it, authors are flattered to be quoted.

At 11:02 came a note from Myrna Kostash in Thessalonica, Greece, where she was immersed in St. Demitrius celebrations: "One icon procession down, three Matins, four Vigils, one Epitaphios, and one Divine liturgy to go" (my head sang along, *and a partridge in a pear tree*). She couldn't help me with the man on the bus.

At 11:50 Luise Denman in Knowlton, Quebec wrote, "Your poet is easy — Lewis Carroll. When did you last read *Alice in Wonderland?*"

As lunch hour ended, Glen Sorestad, our province's poet laureate, wrote that the verse did sound Chestertonish, but had I considered Hilaire Belloc?

At 1:11, Garry Romuldietz, a Saskatoon postal carrier home from his morning round, confirmed Lewis Carroll as the author, and added the poem's title: "The Mad Gardener's Song."

Twenty minutes later Les Dickson in Prince Albert re-confirmed Carroll, and provided a web site with further information.

At 2:21 Trudy Harder from the Frances Morrison Library downtown added another address, along with publication data for Carroll's book. She called my request a blessing to a librarian avoiding deadlines — it was barely 2:00 PM, and she'd already earned two beers that day.

Gerry Hill in Regina hadn't yet heard that I'd received my information, and at 6:00 o'clock suggested that perhaps I was looking for Ogden Nash. And later that evening, Dave Margoshes, the library's writer-in-residence, proposed Nash too, or possibly Thurber.

My Grandpa Gliege would have called it *Hexerei*.

A few days later my granddaughter Katy phoned from Winnipeg, where she was enrolled in kindergarten. She had often sent e-mails like this: *der grapa looyd ramebr wen you kam to or hoes last time you kam i was littl katy xoxo* But her voice on the phone sounded sheepish: "Our computer is broken, and my mom won't let me explain. Could you maybe send me an e-mail in my outside mailbox?"

She induced a mood in me to dig out some letters from the long stretch between the village post office and the new millennium.

There, in my father's thick pencil strokes, from my callow years as a minister and he farming his beloved

Springfield land: "We appritiated your phone call very much, we'll have to do that too sometime."

A note from a high school student who had been in a youth group in my second church: "I went to sit beside the Red River one day, and when I started writing some people came to fish, so I had to go. Otherwise I would have wrote alot sooner." And from her kid sister — gone too soon, alas, from this world: "How are you? I'm fine as possible. I went to Fall camp and had a ball, except I met my ex-boyfriend and he got mad and tried to make me have a terrible time, but I ignored him."

From a university student, an evangelical young man indeed: "Last year I did a project for you that was borrowed from another course. I'm ashamed that when you asked if I had done it, I openly lied. The Lord has been speaking to me about this for a long time."

From an artist more rounded than she knew: "I've finished my first year of teaching. I worked so hard to get here and now can't imagine another year at it. I'd rather be singing rhythm-and-blues, chasing UFOs or hanging out in a cafe. For the first time in my life, I don't know where I'm going, or what I want."

And around the time of my own leavetaking blues, I had received a note in hand-printed capital letters from a former parishioner two weeks before his unexpected death: "WRITING TO LET YOU KNOW I AM THINKING OF YOU AND WONDERING JUST HOW YOU ARE MAKING OUT FROM DAY TO DAY."

Tidings of a poet's hippopotamus. Reminders to read Lewis Carroll. Mail saying howdy — hope you're having a ball.

What the Soul Knows

What is it in the soul, then, which makes it take more pleasure
in the finding or recovery of things it loves than in the
continual possession of them?

— St. Augustine

JUNGIAN THERAPISTS MARIE-LOUISE VON FRANZ and
James Hall write that, although the human psyche does
not ignore physical death, it regards it in dream and
imagination as merely another event to go through,
beyond which some form of life always persists. It's as
if the soul knows her states, and cannot envision non-
being.

Hall and von Franz write of a dying person who
dreams that a great tree is cut down. Immediately a new
sprout appears from the stump. Another dreams that a
candle in the windowsill burns out; instantly it appears,
re-lit, on the outside. Many people return from clinical
death with reports of tunnels and lights, and experiences
ranging from infernal to sublime — and regardless of
formal religious involvement, or lack of it. We ourselves
may dream of our death, and be nonetheless present at

the funeral; or of departed friends who appear alive and vigorous, yet we feel no conflict or oddity as the dream continues.

In Greek mythology, Hypnos and Thanatos are the deities of sleep and death, and they are twin brothers. Spiritual traditions (which depth psychology considers as the upward, pneumatic tendencies of soul) typically regard sleep as a small death, death as a great sleep; and they urge us therefore to see what can happen even in our nightly passings.

A year after my father's death, one night I lay in bed half-awake, and began feeling the peculiar vibrations Robert Monroe describes in his classic study of "out-of-body experiences". At first, the pulses were minimal and pleasant, and I tried to go with them, much the way a child rides a swing, or we "help" a car to get unstuck; but then the surges grew intense, and one was so strong that it jolted me awake.

I got up, wondering how to account for these experiences I'd occasionally begun having, which occupied me partly for their accompanying ecstasies, but also for what they suggested about psychological possibilities beyond mere skepticism and mere belief.

I sat up a while, then went back to bed hoping the pulsations might return; and I did sense them — quite physically — but again, they either remained too feeble, or became so overwhelming that they startled me back to the bedroom. And eventually I gave up my designs, and drifted to sleep.

I didn't know then that I was dreaming as I pedalled a bicycle through my childhood village. There was the little crocus meadow beside the elevators. There, in the window of the shoe-shop, John Ziegelman worked at his oversized treadle machine, cigarette holder clamped in his yellowed teeth. I passed the village well with its old pump, and turned along a street where my father's friend and hunting companion lived.

As I neared his house, he came stumbling outside as if drunk, and sat down on the grass. I turned into his lane to say hello — and suddenly Dad himself was on the sidewalk, and I knew at once that this was a dream: Dad had died, I was asleep, and we were in a "dimension between life and death" — the words were given with the dream itself, not as later conjecture or interpretation.

I dropped the bicycle and ran to Dad, overjoyed to see him. We embraced, and I felt the sharp stubble of his beard graze my cheek. I was electrified to know that a dream-body could be so solid, *more* solid even than anything I knew in the other, "waking", life.

The troubled friend on the lawn stirred and got up; but I wanted urgently to know what Dad had been doing since we last met, and asked him about it. He said he kept busy with many things, and still went to work for a few hours each day. I wanted to ask what kinds of jobs he did — but now I woke up, it seemed, in bed. I reached for a pen to record the dream, as was my custom; but in a process of backward association I recalled an earlier one, and began writing it down first. Then continued with the bicycle ride in the village — and abruptly I was back in the intermediate dimension, but standing now in my parents' front yard with Dad and his younger brother.

The lucidity had returned with a surge. Here was a realm between life and death, and I entreated the brothers, "Please, let's do things slowly, I want to remember them."

Yet like a doubting Thomas, I ran my fingers over Dad's face again, felt the muscles of his shoulders and the silk of his greying hair, to assure myself of his substantiality; and again found him really, truly present. With that, I recalled the vibrations I'd felt while falling asleep, and announced gleefully to the others, "I made it out after all!"

Without ado, Dad and I took to the air at great speed, and streaked up to dizzying altitudes. I called after my uncle to come and join us, but he stayed below on the sidewalk. I turned again toward Dad, and saw him vanishing so rapidly that in a blink he had become a speck in the distance, and was gone.

A vast loneliness overcame me, and I called frantically, *Dad! Dad!* but quickly realized he wouldn't return. I flew on alone for a time, but the joy was gone; and now I saw that the sky had darkened, too. There was no use calling out so anxiously, and I lowered my voice and said calmly, *Dad* — so clearly that as I awakened, I was sure the word must have been audible in the external room.

In a state of near reverence, I began anew to write things down — and with another jolt realized that both this and the previous "awakening" had been illusions. Now I *was* aroused, though by comparison with what I had just left, it hardly seemed an awakening. Already the images threatened to fade, and I took the pen again, tried to return to the beginning and scribble the events as I recalled them.

In the morning I wrote them out, wistfully. And there was no need to make-believe that the soul is all that it knows.

QUEEN OF CLUBS

MAYDAY! Our mother's neighbour calls to say that Mom looks bad, very bad; she's been out making a garden, but something has gone awry and an ambulance is coming to take her to the Rosthern Hospital. By the time we drive out from the city, she's strapped in an emergency room wheelchair, moaning *Ohh, ohh,* lifting hands alternately to her forehead, or gripping the chair's edge and straining to get out. Her eyes seem to see, but she doesn't respond to us, and we can only repeat the things we most want her to know: *We love you; please try to rest; everyone is helping; things will be all right* — and try to believe this last ourselves.

The doctor on duty arranges a transfer to Saskatoon's Royal University Hospital. I ride back with Mom in the ambulance, and she calms somewhat; but at the new emergency ward she rears and thrashes again, jabs her feet through the bedrails as if determined to get up and leave. Eventually a CT scan shows bacteria from an ear infection eating through the mastoid into the meningi between her skull and brain, and already spreading into the right temporal lobe. Air pockets generate internal pressure and make her head ache ferociously. No one will estimate the brain damage without neurological tests, and she's not conscious enough to respond.

At eighty-five, our mother still claims never to get tired but for some occasional eye-strain; she maintains her own acreage, walks easily ten or fifteen kilometres a day, and keeps a calendar so full that we can't necessarily see her when we want. She's dubbed "Mother Theresa of Laird": chauffeur for the immobile, cook and deliverer of meals, pianist for church and community events, baby-sitter for kids who call her Grandma Elsie — in another day she might have been labelled hyperactive, and we hope this lifelong dynamism will aid her now. Finally she settles for the night, but next morning is "combative" again — strange accusatory word for someone said to be unconscious — and it takes three nurses to subdue and medicate her.

We siblings are confounded by specialists coming and going, and in the first two days are asked half a dozen times whether we want Mom resuscitated "if something should happen". Yes, we say — until we know more, how can we say otherwise? They predict that her hearing will be gone, though some may return if she survives. Her memory and other cognitive functions (but which ones?) will certainly be affected. Some doctors are resolved to prepare us for the worst; others confine themselves to statistics: a certain percentage of similar cases die, a few recover fully, and in between are disabilities ranging from minor to severe.

We stare at Mom across the bedrail to see whether she's still breathing, as she once stood beside our cribs, and we did at our own children's: *Are you still here?* Her head turns, her eyes open and we think *She's back!* but next instant see differently —there is no recognition. Three antibiotics flow through plastic lines into her deranged body. Finally the white blood-cell count drops slightly, and we hope it means the infection is contained. Days and nights begin blurring together. We practically live at the hospital, to be there if she wakes up, there if she dies.

Near the end of the week, her eyes snap to attention; scan, stop, follow our faces. She swallows and half-smiles. Where she had measured seven on the coma-scale (fifteen being "awake"), now she reaches ten, and maintains the level for a day. Propped up in bed, she's particularly wide-eyed as we play a tape of her favourite music. Then again, the eyes are blank — but where has she gone?

On Mothers' Day weekend, the seizures begin. Her upper body convulses, one arm jerks erratically, her face contorts and she breathes in laboured gasps. Each spasm lasts a couple of minutes, and in the intervals she sleeps, making loud exasperated sounds. A dozen doctors are involved now with this "unusual case". Meningitis is more common in children, they say, yet not many elders have our mother's stamina. But one physician repeats several times, "She's very sick, very sick."

While the nurses suction, pummel, and turn her, I walk through the basement of an old hospital wing, into a cramped tunnel I didn't know was here. Gigantic pipes crowd my head, and signs warn of asbestos. Every so often a dark cubicle appears on the left, its shadows shifting as I approach — another stairwell to the College of Medicine above. A single playing-card, the Queen of

Clubs, lies on the floor. I pick her up and ascend from the tunnel, and emerge in a corridor where signs on offices advertise the specialties of each medical worker. I sit in a lounge and stare out at the grey buildings, grey clouds. Not a doctor here on the weekend; only a distant pair of footsteps slapping the clean tiles, and the hum of Coke's big upright machine. I miss the old red icebox in Don's Store when I was a kid, pulling up stubby glass bottles and snapping off the caps — *Pfftt* — on the recessed opener, frosty drops spilling to the wooden floorboards.

By the next day Mom's seizures last five minutes each; on the coma scale she sinks to four, and a note on her chart reads, "Does not respond to pain." We speak tenderly in her ear: *We're here with you, Mom. You're always in our hearts.*

The seizures become continuous, with rare half-minute reprieves, and they are reclassified *grand mal*. Three new medications are administered; one after another they fail, and the wreckage escalates. A seventh, phenobarbitol, leaves her quiet, chest rising and falling rhythmically. We keep repeating, *We love you; please don't be afraid.* Or we recite Psalms: *Yea, though I walk through the valley of the shadow of death, I will fear no evil . . .*

At the beginning of the second week, the hospital's senior neurologist takes five minutes to "see" their meningitis patient, and relays a message through the nurse: "Give mama a valium drip and let her go." Within an hour, a palliative care team arrives to discuss moving her to St. Paul's Hospital. We children grope in the thick mist between "active treatment" and "provision of comfort". We look up the word *palliate:* "to reduce the violence of a disease." We don't want our mother beat up any more; she's fought the good fight. A miracle can happen, we suppose, on the west side of the river as well as here, among researchers and interns.

Around midnight a bed becomes available, and Mom's inert body is transported to St. Paul's. All medications will be reduced or withdrawn. She lies now at the mercies of a new and exceptionally kind staff, looking indeed as if she has gone to still waters and green pastures. I try to see everything twice — once for Mom, once for me.

But these workers with the sick and the dying, do they find it any easier to die themselves?

Third week. Mom runs a fever during the withdrawal, and a few mild seizures recur. Our nuclear family dysfunctions flare into the open — our fear and rage, the sad orphanages of our minds. We all need palliation. We take turns sleeping on a pull-out as the oxygen hose bubbles at the head of Mom's bed, and try to recall her face without this mask, a face that met us at the door laughing *Ha ha ha, this is great!* that whirled in and out of rooms, *Boy, we're having a good time!*

Then near the end of May, a bodily resurrection begins. Mom clears her throat and sneezes. Her lip curls. She opens her eyes and blinks. Wiggles the fingers of one hand, and squeezes ours. She murmurs at the rainbow beyond her window; shakes her head at the sight of a flower, "Oh, isn't that beautiful!" — the words come out clear as a belltone.

Over the next few days, she enters our world and leaves it again, much as we go in and out of our dreams. One side of her body is paralyzed, but she smiles most of the time she's awake, new eyes flashing blue in the south window's light. Or she startles and puzzles, and quickly turns happy again. I read aloud from her old diary: *May 10, 1937 — Washed and planted potatoes,* and ask incredulously, "You washed dirt *off* the potatoes before putting them *in* dirt?" and she giggles like a kid.

I look across the room at her, and she forms her mouth into an O, and extends her tongue like a birdling. I give her a few drops of water and she says, "Thank you for all your help." I weep; she strokes my face with the one hand that moves. My mother is a re-born child; and she's an elder embodying gratitude, joy, serenity — God grant me such serenity. Her face looks younger than it did at Easter, when she hosted her tribe and led us in singing the Doxology as we sat to her table, and consumed the meal too hastily.

One day we hear that Kathy and Abe, Mom's neighbours who had placed the *Mayday* calls at the beginning, are coming to visit the hospital. They've already tended to her garden and mowed her acreage without being asked. I tell Mom that we'll get a thank-you gift on her behalf, and though she can't speak just then, a tear forms in her eye and falls to the pillow.

As I return from my errand, the westering sun lights up 20th Street from end to end. There's been new rain, and the world is as green as creation day. I park near the hospital again. At the front door on a sturdy concrete base, Jesus with open arms welcomes me.

A Catholic statue never looked so good.

The next six months are volatile for our mother. Rapid changes — some heartening, many oppressive —

transform her from the lively creature she had been, to a shut-in devastated in mind and body. After further shuttlings around emergency wards and hospitals and assessment units, with a legion of experts doing as they would, Mom has settled, finally, in her room in a nursing home.

Settled? She's locked there, with a mind that goes whither and hence, and a body that sits or lies as the attendants place it, and often in great pain, this body that till the *Mayday* hardly knew what to do with its steam.

She hears and understands, even the medical people agree; but she is largely paralyzed, and the meagre speech left after the meningitis attack slowly deserts her now. Occasionally a clear phrase escapes — *Hey, mister!* she calls when the doctor comes around; and there's the odd moment of levity, at least for us, when she protests: *Oh for pete snakes!* But many of her remaining words — *yes, no, thank-you* — are there unfaithfully, along with a few erroneous names by which she calls relatives and friends alike. Sometimes we infer her meaning from the bright smiles she still musters, or from her tears when she despairs of being understood.

I visit her often, feel sad and negligent when I don't, though I'm helpless to add an hour to her life or subtract one minute of pain. Whether I sit with her over a meal, or keep late-evening vigil, it comes to the same thing: not enough. I wheel her around the hallways in a Broda chair, once in awhile kiss the back of her head — the drugs have made most of her hair fall out — and park in the sunniest lounge I can find, try to get a grip, and repeat what Wally at the palliative ward said the dying (and who isn't?) long to hear: *I love you. Please forgive me.*

I forgive you. I'll be all right. Or we sit quietly in her room and commune by candlelight, our tears and silence more profound anyway than words. And yet, when the queen of clout reaches out the one semi-functional arm in a crook to hug her son, it's a benediction no old-time religion ever gave.

Pascal said that most human problems stem from an inability to sit by ourselves in our rooms. But Mom's "cure" is too drastic, while I still go too fast and without knowing where. I drive from the nursing home in her car, which I use these days, and turn up a blues album on the stereo — *Damn right,* somebody wails, *you damn right I've got the blues.*

How dumb the stuffed bunny hangs by a thumb-tack on the wall of my mother's room. How bare the prairie stretches around her empty house in the late November afternoon.

TICKET TO HEAVEN

SHE LOOKED LIKE A LITTLE BIRD in the hospital bed — beak, claws, and wisps of hair above the sheet, bones underneath raising hardly a bump.

She was the aunt who had rocked me to sleep in her Springfield farmhouse, when I was an infant and my home had burned down. Later she "step-mothered" my sisters and me when we lived across the garden from her and Grandpa at the edge of the village, and we spent as much time at their place as at ours. And when our Mom was ravaged by meningitis and put in a nursing home, Aunt Anne "mothered" her younger sister too, and us aging children as always, until at the age of ninety-five she fell on her stairs and broke her hip.

She had moved from farm to village to city, and been hale and sturdy all her life; but when she reached her early nineties (declining as ever to reveal her age), she began saying that she didn't want to live much longer.

My sister found her on the basement floor of her house. She had lain there for more than a day, but in her delirium insisted that she'd just now been reading from the New Testament book of *Romans*. And waiting in the emergency ward for surgery, she complained that some people were saying she had broken her hip. "It's just a made-up story," she protested. Of all her morphine-induced sayings, this was what she repeated most often: someone has made this up.

She had earlier shown us the dresser drawer where she kept her box of "important papers", and as her powers-of-attorney we had found a neatly-written note among them: *Please do not resuscitate, Anne.*

She came through the surgery without the least complication, but not two weeks later when I went to visit one day, she said, "I tell you, it's no good to get old." Hardly three days later she spied me from her wheel-chair in the hallway, and asked without even a hello: "Tell me, is life worth living?" And within the week had concluded, apparently, that it was not. My sister had called from St. Paul's to say that Aunt Anne was gravely ill, and that our middle sister was on her way into the city. But when I entered the hospital room, I was stunned at how small our aunt had become.

I touched her arm, and she stirred. I said, "I've come to thank you for the hundredth time for the love you gave me long ago, and have always given."

The arm rose slightly, and fell to the bed again. Her eyelids fluttered, but did not — could not — open.

I thanked her for the bedtime stories she had read me as a kid, and for scratching my back; for the mornings she let me stay warm under the quilt as she shook the grate down in the kitchen, and lit a fire with scraps from Grandpa's workshop, and made porridge and johnny-cake for breakfast.

I asked forgiveness for my shortcomings; asked her not to be afraid — but it was my own fear speaking. Her left arm made sporadic motions; whether they were meant as gestures, I could not say. For some minutes my sister and I took turns stroking the aged hand, holding it in our own.

Then, with no sound, her eyes opened. For a long minute they stayed riveted on the floor beneath the window — utterly, fearlessly open, and (though the thought seemed overbold) even astonished. The breaths grew laboured, and fell farther apart. Her eyes closed again. She began to retch, and spilled the last of what she'd taken in — reluctantly, but so obligingly — at others' coaxings. There was breath, and there wasn't; and a gentle soul had suspired.

Nurses came running to check her vital signs. "She went so fast," they said, and shooed us urgently into the hall to let them clean the little body on the bed.

When we were allowed back into the room again, we lowered the bedrails and sat and talked with our aunt, and with each other, and wished our sister could have been there. It was the first time I had seen someone die. Silently, I asked the chariot to swing by our mother's nursing home and take her aboard too.

Aunt Anne kept a tidy house. We were the executors of the estate, and one day sorted through her things to claim a few treasures in her memory. There was a spice cabinet my Grandfather had built, that still smelled of childhood's black peppercorns; and one of his wooden trunks in which she had kept letters and doilies, and plastic flowers from occasions known only to herself. I rescued a red tomato pin-cushion from her sewing room, and a little case that snapped shut on rings of keys that opened nothing.

Eventually the day came when I spent several hours with charity workers emptying the house of Aunt Anne's remaining possessions. Everything fit into one load, and the truck pulled away in the late afternoon with a broom and a dry mop sticking out through the tailgate.

I wandered through the house in silence. A few things had been left behind. In the spare room was a rickety davenport on which she had lately slept to be nearer her bathroom. A houseplant on the floor still struggled to live, and I watered it and set it on the kitchen counter to get the next day's sun. The dead ones I put in a place of their own.

In the basement, many scraps of lumber still remained. Some had been used as stakes for garden plants, a few as shims under her appliances; but there were boxes and bucketfuls of no use that I could see — saved, perhaps, from habit's necessity like leftovers from her father's workshop, though she no longer had a wood-burning stove.

I lingered in the middle of the floor at the spot where she had crawled after the accident, where my sister had found her. I knew the place by its blood-stains. I stood under an obscure cloud of things undone, while overhead the fluorescent light buzzed in monotone.

There were a few cardboard boxes, too. One contained old games and jigsaw puzzles. From an unfamiliar board-game I drew out a card that read *PERMIT TO HEAVEN*, capital letters arched over a pair of wrought-iron gates, and tiny crosses sprinkled like stars in the background. The ticket was bordered with King James Bible texts: *Christ died for our sins according to the scriptures . . . He that hath the Son hath life . . . The blood of Jesus Christ cleanseth us from all sin . . .*

I slipped the permit into my pocket as if committing a sacrilege — I might need it some day — and began climbing the stairs. Aunt Annie had done her dying; she didn't have to die any more.

REQUIEM

I have a gentil cock Croweth me day; He doth me risen early
My matins for to say.

        —Anonymous fifteenth-century poet

Lauds

Summer 1973. We turn from the Trans-Canada Highway onto the Yellowhead, and a little red car whizzes past us and disappears over a rise. A moment later we follow, and in the flat panorama, with prairie towns visible on both sides, a long freight train is crossing the highway; and we pull up where warnings clang and flash at the intersection. The train is lumbering to a stop, too, with the engine halfway to Portage la Prairie when the brakes squeal their last, long protest.

We sit with the car idling. In the back seat, our two-year-old daughter teases her infant sister. They don't understand that their parents' marriage is already troubled. Something sticks up from the wheatfield beside the road, and I remark that it looks like a piece of farm implement fallen off a flatdeck.

After five minutes I switch off the motor.

The conductor heads forward from the caboose, and in the distance we see the engineer descend from the cab and begin making his way back. A dozen vehicles are stalled behind us now. A few drivers get out to stretch. One leaves a radio playing, and the Eagles come drifting on the summer air, *Peaceful easy feeling*.

I get out of the car and chat with a few others. A man and a woman begin wading through the wheat toward the middle of the train. I go to join them, and we wonder why the railcars aren't split to let us through while the fallen equipment is salvaged.

As we come within earshot, the engineer's voice crackles through a two-way radio: "Is anyone alive back there?"

The conductor coughs and replies, "No. There's only one, but he's dead."

The body lies face up beside the steel rail, fully clothed and scarcely mangled. Only the jaw has been torn off. The dead man's tongue rises from its root in the throat, and hangs down toward a wooden railway tie. Black flies crawl in and out at a vertical crack in the forehead. There is no trace of a car except the axle protruding from the grain near the highway — what I had mistaken for farm machinery.

The engineer has called for help even before stopping the train. He says this is not the first time he's seen something like this. We stand in clumsy silence, with only the flies buzzing into the head and out again. Eventually we hear a siren wail faintly. An ambulance turns into the wheatfield with a police cruiser close behind, and they hurry toward us.

The cops get out and size things up. "A Smith & Wesson beats four aces," one says, "but can't nobody beat a train." And he dismisses the bystanders: "We'll take over. You can return to your vehicles."

The other couple's heads are down as they follow the diagonal trail back through the grain. I set out along the embankment toward the highway, and look over my shoulder. The police make notes. The attendants load the body on a stretcher, and cover it. A breeze riffles the wheat beside the silent train.

In the car, our daughters play and giggle in the back seat. We see the ambulance leave slowly through the field. Finally the train is opened, and we drive on toward Riding Mountain, checking the newscasts every half-hour but hearing nothing.

That night evil spirits infest the bedroom. I ponder the sermon I will give to my congregation on Sunday. I get up and write a lament for our headlong career through life, until some grim hand concludes our hopeful designs. The Eagles still whisper in my ear — tell me that someone will never see anyone else again.

Prime

Fall 1955, village of Laird. In the parlour, the relatives sit beside Grandma Gliege's deathbed. I watch and listen through eight-year-old eyes and ears. Aunt Wanda clings tearfully to hope: *Vielleicht ist sie nicht tot,* maybe she's not dead, maybe she's in a coma. *Ach nein,* Grandpa's voice is resigned. And he tells how she raised her hands, asked to be lifted higher, and called loudly *Mein Heiland, mein Heiland* — Saviour, my saviour — and passed away.

There is talk about whether she might have seen a vision of Christ.

Calls are made from the party-line telephone behind the kitchen door. The doctor is summoned from Rosthern, and the undertaker from Dalmeny. Grandma is pronounced dead. My dad and three uncles roll her in a blanket, sling the ends over their shoulders, and lug her heavily toward the front porch. Halfway through the living room I hear a great gush of water from the body onto the floor — the men pause and renew their grip, and continue out to the hearse parked at the gate.

After the funeral service, Grandma's coffin is carried from the Salem country church out to the cemetery. The pallbearers' ties flap in the prairie wind. A sister from Kansas hasn't arrived in time but is expected the following day. The casket is left on the ground, tilted slightly toward the grave, to watch over itself through the night.

Next morning there are other readings and prayers. The men lower the grey box into the earth on long canvas straps, cover it with a wooden panel, and begin shovelling. The rocks bounce on the lid and I look hastily around at nearby headstones saying, *Better in Glory than down here, Safe through the blood of Jesus, The Lord is my Shepherd Shall not want* (the *I* is missing); and over the remains of another eight-year-old, *Suffer the little children*.

In spring Grandpa puts up a new monument, chisels letters into the concrete with tools from his own workshop: *Ruhe Sanft*, rest gently.

Terce

Summer 1956. Across the road and east of Salem, there is a deep dugout half-surrounded by a poplar bush. My cousin and I cross the pasture at her farm, keep one eye on the bull grazing in the far corner and the other on cowpies in the grass. Safely past, we come to four cement slabs, big as the bases of statues, leading into the dugout. The first lies flat on the ground, the second slopes down a bit, the third is half in and half out of the water, and the last one knee-deep in the dugout, with a raft tied to a post beside it. The farthest pad shimmers underwater in the sun, and beyond it are mud and weeds and murky depths.

We are here with a Rogers' Syrup pail to catch things from the dugout, mostly snails and tadpoles. She dips, pulls up five snails. We scoop them out, fat little pointy black pears, slippery in our fingers. And line them up on the cement.

My turn. I lean over the water, and fetch up three more. Six snails make an L — four down and two across. Her turn again. Twelve snails for two Ls: one for Lorraine, one for Lloyd. We throw the tadpoles back.

A calf bawls beside the fence. The cow butts it away. A cricket begins to hum, and sings along the barbed wire until petering out.

Lorraine's turn, nine shiny snails this time, she's getting good at it. Enough for an O and one left over for an R.

How many snails spell our names?

Ripples from the dugout lap faintly at the concrete. The grass is fresh. A girl smells good, better than her brothers who shove me off the raft. Once, I thought I'd die down in the slime, and barely made it to shore while they hooted from across the water.

No brothers here now. No preachers.

Deep blue sky reaches up as far as it can. *This world is not my home, I'm just a-passing through,* we sing in Salem, there on the other side of the bush, along the correction line. The church feels sleepy when you go inside on a weekday.

A plump toad takes a hop beside the grass. It was invisible, now it sits there. Six snails for another L, eight for an O, we share the snails, finish our names. *Angels beckon me from heaven's open door, I can't feel at home in this world any more . . .*

Letters shifting, squirming in slow motion. A breeze travels over the dugout, through the bush and out to the road. At the church it becomes a dust devil, *Dust thou art, and to dust thou shalt return,* they said when our Grandma died and they buried her at the back of the churchyard.

Sun standing still, names at the end of the cement, snails dropping one by one into the water again.

Sext

Winter Sunday afternoon, 1998, Saskatoon. Winnie erupts in a rage at her husband of fifty years, claws his face as he tries to stop her from leaving the apartment, and throws an open bottle of antacid over him before escaping down the hall and pounding at the neighbours' doors. She doesn't recognize Ian again, and he comes and rouses us from sleep, and simultaneously we hear Winnie's commotion in the hallway.

The medication has bloated her face, and she is frantic. She demands, "Someone do something about this asshole instead of just standing there talking!" One tenant, a social worker, tries unsuccessfully to soothe her, and when she storms back to our end of the building I suggest mildly that maybe she'd like to sleep awhile — hoping the image of her bed might comfort her. But she turns her back and strides into her apartment cursing: "You can go to hell — all of you are the same!" and locks us out: doorknob, deadbolt, and chain.

Someone phones Betty, the caretaker, who comes from the adjacent building. She has helped Winnie before, and now begins coaxing her patiently to open the door. Ian sits in our living room and cries, says again and again that he wants us to know he hasn't done anything to hurt his wife. He reminisces about their old house on a nearby avenue, which he built himself, built so solidly that it will stand long after the houses around it have fallen. He speaks of the business he operated, and of raising children, and finally of moving into the suite across the hall and being happy there for twenty years. He recalls Winnie's keen mind and trim body even into her eighties, and her tart humour, all of which we've seen for ourselves in the decade we have been their neighbours; and then a few months ago — a year at most — the onset of Winnie's illness, and her rapid disintegration. "She's not herself," Ian says, and sobs as he renews his determination to put her in a care home. But what will become of him, then, with his crippling arthritis and his own ailing health?

The Mobile Crisis team arrives. They look around and say they can't do anything, and leave. Betty phones a son of Winnie's and Ian's across the city. He won't come.

After an hour, Betty taps on our door to say that Winnie has wandered into her bedroom but isn't yet ready for sleep. We smuggle Ian back to the apartment, hoping that when she comes to the living room again she'll remember him.

She does. In a moment the two have fallen on each other with hugs and kisses, and Ian practically giggling in relief, and I wonder how he can sustain his resolve to put her into care.

Winnie is not herself — not even the self is immortal. Who is she, then?

None

Fall 2000. Salem cemetery. Ripe sun in the clean September light. I've come to visit my recently buried cousin, Judi. A poplar leaf drifts toward my father's tombstone. To the left, a fresh mound of earth is piled beside an open pit. A backhoe waits behind the carra-ganas. The procession will arrive soon.

Passing by the new grave I look down: at the bottom, so small among scraped dirt walls, a plain grey-floral casket like my Grandmother's fifty years ago, not a real petal on its lid — nor, when I look again, on the ground above. Stark hole in the prairie: the machine man hasn't had time, he'll get here, he'll get here. *And what if a badger gnaws through the coffin,* I think, *what if the corpse pushes on the lid and sits up, what if I fall on top of that corpse?*

Vespers

Fall 2001. A dream. Two women have come to visit Salem cemetery, where their ancestors are buried. They've dug up three caskets which are still above ground; they want to bury them again, but offer to show me the remains before they do.

These relatives have been dead for a hundred years, and I expect to see only skeletons. The coffins are homemade pine boxes, warped and discoloured but otherwise intact. The women open the first lid. The body inside is decayed beyond recognition, though patches of leathered flesh cling to the bones. It lies toward the head of the casket, as if having been jostled and crowded forward at the burial. The women hold their noses, and I step upwind.

The second corpse is also badly decomposed. It lies doubled over, as if the dying person had been in great pain to the end.

When the women open the third casket, I'm dumbfounded to see that on the inside it resembles a tiny room. A young girl sits against the wall, pale but immaculately preserved, staring at three small statuettes in her hand. Then she begins to sing, and I am transported in rapture, and return scarcely in time to hear the plainsong ending in her dulcet tones: *The angels like to live here too,* she sings; and in the repose that follows, is lost again in her vision of heralds in the figurines.

I fear to disturb her, but murmur in spite of myself, "Have a nice dream, dear girl."

She looks up and says, "I don't know who you are."

"I'm a friend," I say, "have a nice dream." And as I turn from the grave, a dove flies across the way and circles the dugout where we other children once spelled our names in snails.

Compline

Spring 2002, Saskatoon. I cross a channel on stepping-stones to an island in the South Saskatchewan River. Beside the willow saplings lies a plastic grocery bag, neatly tied, plainly not left as garbage. In the bag, a child's drawing of its family is wrapped around a cookie box. And inside the box, a white washcloth lines the cardboard, shrouds a brown hamster with folded paws — as nearly folded as they can be.

My curiosity doesn't know what to do after disturbing a pet's casket.

But the animal must not lie here, it must be set adrift, like a little Moses on the Nile, and have words spoken over it: "You have died, but the hamster-spirit hasn't gone anywhere. And you are that." I push the box out into the current, for a moment watch it bob in the waves, and retrace my steps home.

The next evening toward sunset, I cross the channel again. Downstream, the plastic bag lies washed up on the sand. Farther along, the little ark has come aground, too, bent crooked from its voyage. There is no white cloth, no family picture. And the body, after its own fashion, has gone to the skies.

We are always children, obliged to walk away.

EPILOGUE

WHEN BALLPOINT PENS FIRST APPEARED in the Laird School, our principal regarded them as abominations, and swiftly decreed their banishment: "Pen and ink here on Monday!" — it wasn't a suggestion but a commandment. And however we underlings liked to defy him then, I concede that fountain pens are more elegant than ballpoints: for *fountain* pleases the eardrum, and the nib scratches satisfyingly on the paper. Back in the fourth grade, there was always a bottle of Quink or Waterman's under the desktop; and when it dwindled, Don's Store had another one; and when his shelf was bare, the train from Saskatoon replenished it on Thursday — the inkwell, so far as I know, never ran dry.

I believe we readers and writers are engaged in reversing our incarnations. We restore the world to word. But why?

From the writer's side, something presses out, pushes toward expression. And if the act of writing is not itself a pretty sight (as Christopher Lehmann-Haupt observes), yet the state of *having written* is one of the most blissful known to humans, rivalling even sex or religious rapture. From the reader's side, there is a search for communion: the joy of discovering that someone has voiced our experience, and we are not alone; or disappointment that life has *not* been well-expressed, so we read on, or try to write it ourselves. And on the divine side, it's said, in the beginning is the Word that means God — nothing in itself until pressed-out, formulated. Word becomes flesh, and flesh re-creates words, our human pluralism tending back toward singularity, and the trinity itself, perhaps, returning to the peace of union.

I believe in the communion of words.

Reversing one's incarnation does not imply that the "forwardness" of creation is a mistake. An infant is born *(once in royal David's city, in a lowly cattle shed)* and who will say that the movement is wrongly directed? And if the mature person reverts to word, how can it be called an error the other way? We are back-and-forth creatures, *in caro,* carnivorous, eating up the world for the sake of word.

This evening I drive back toward the city in a Courtney Milne landscape. Passenger jets like silver fountain pens trace their signatures on the blue vellum dome. The tips of Wanuskewin's architecture protrude just above the plain. The eastern horizon at sunset is too exquisite — my word-palette lacks such hues, alack.

I kiss the joy.

It flies.

NOTES

Every reasonable effort has been made to contact holders of copyrighted material. The author will gladly correct inadvertent omissions on receipt of further information.

pp 23,24 & 28: The lyrics are from Lee Roy Abernathy's "A Wonderful Time Up There".

p 40: The epigraph attributed to Hughes Mearns is variously titled "Antigonish", "The Psychoed", and "The Little Man". The latter version, cited here, is from *The New Oxford Book of Children's Verse,* edited by Neil Philip (Oxford University Press, 1996).

p 45: Philip Rieff, *The Triumph of the Therapeutic: Uses of Faith After Freud* (Harper & Row, 1968).

pp 45-48: Quotations from Charles Templeton's *Anecdotal Memoir* (McClelland and Stewart, 1983) and *Act of God* (McClelland and Stewart-Bantam Seal, 1978) are reprinted with the kind permission of Madeleine Templeton.

p 49: John Redwood-Anderson's poem "Divine Appointment" first appeared in Raynor C. Johnson, *Watcher on the Hills* (Hodder and Stoughton, 1959). The publisher has no record of copyright ownership.

p 50: The epigraph is from #117 in *Emily Dickinson*, Laurel Poetry Series (Dell, 1960).

pp 50-51: John Neihardt, *Black Elk Speaks* (Washington Square Press, 1959). Quotations reprinted by permission of the University of Nebraska Press.

p 53: See "World" entry in J. P. Cirlot's *Dictionary of Symbols* (Philosophical Library, 1971).

p 54: The epigraph is from Elemire Zolla, *Archetypes: The Persistence of Unifying Patterns* (Harcourt, Brace, Jovanovich, 1981). My abridgement of Ambrose Bierce's definition is from *The Devil's Dictionary* (American Century Series, Hill and Wang, 1961).

p 55: Northrop Frye, *The Great Code: The Bible and Literature* (Academic Press Canada, 1982).

pp 55-57: Boehme's works are in the public domain. These citations are from *The Confessions of Jacob Boehme,* edited by W. Scott Palmer (Harper & Brothers, 1954).

p 58: Walt Whitman, "Song of Myself". *The Portable Walt Whitman* (Viking Press, 1945).

p 69: Jolande Jacobi, *Complex/Archetype/Symbol in the Psychology of C. G. Jung.* Bollingen Series LVII (Princeton University Press, 1959).

p 72: The Tennyson reference is to "Choric Song" in *A Choice of Tennyson's Verse* (Faber and Faber, 1971).

p 74: Lines from Holan's poem "To the Enemy" appear on pp 54 & 55 of *Vladimir Holan: Selected Poems* (Harmondsworth, Middlesex, England, Copyright © Vladimir Holan, 1971; translation copyright © Jarmila and Ian Milner, 1971). They are reproduced by permission of Penguin Books Ltd.

p 81: Edward C. Whitmont, *The Symbolic Quest* (Princeton University Press, 1969).

p 93: The allusion is to "An Old Man's Winter Night" from *Robert Frost's Poems* (Washington Square Press, 1967).

p 105: The Rilke epigraph is from Babette Deutsch's translation, *Poems from the Book of Hours* (New Directions Publishing, 1941).

p106: Pascal's "memorial" is described in Evelyn Underhill's *Mysticism* (University Paperbacks, Methuen & Co., 1960).

p 108: The Keats line is from "Hyperion, Book One", in *John Keats: Selected Poetry and Letters* (Holt, Rinehart and Winston, 1962).

p 110: "The Mad Gardener's Song" is from Lewis Carroll's *Sylvie and Bruno*.

p 113: The epigraph is from *The Confessions of St. Augustine*, translated by Rex Warner (New American Library, 1963).

Biblical references throughout are from *The Holy Bible*, commonly known as the Authorized or King James Version of 1611; and from *The New English Bible With the Apocrypha: Oxford Study Edition*, Copyright ©1976 by Oxford University Press, Inc.